Risking His Heart

A SMALL-TOWN CHRISTIAN ROMANCE

CHRISTMAS IN REDEMPTION RIDGE

EMILY CONRAD

Copyright © 2025 by Emily Conrad

Published by Hope Anchor, LLC

PO Box 3091, Oshkosh, WI 54903

Library of Congress Control Number: 2025915084

ISBN 9781957455204 (Paperback Edition)

ISBN 9781957455198 (Ebook Edition)

Edited by Brandi Aquino, Editing Done Write

Proofread by Judy DeVries, Judicious Revisions

Cover designed by Amanda Walker, PA & Design Services

Visit the author's website at EmilyConradAuthor.com.

Chapter One

If good things come to those who wait, Cody was doing something wrong. Perhaps his version of waiting involved too much work. Like a flighty animal, "good things" smelled years' worth of blood, sweat, and tears from a mile off and fled the other direction.

Right there, in the home of a burglary victim, his pen hovered, a few lines from finishing the police report. Maybe it was time to quit trying to make things happen. He could stop being so thorough, since his good reputation had yet to land him a promotion to detective. And he could distance himself from Neenah, who'd locked him in the friend zone years ago.

Except then he'd be left with an empty, miserable existence. Neenah might never return his feelings, but as his best friend, her companionship got him through the day. And promotion or no, the people of Redemption Ridge deserved safety and justice, not cut corners.

He pressed pen to paper and finished his report, then he passed it to Rob Tropes, the homeowner who stood with him at the kitchen counter. "We'll do everything in our power to recover your property."

Rob accepted it blindly as his glazed eyes surveyed the living room beyond the counter.

The biggest sign of anything amiss in the tidy home, besides the empty space where the TV once hung, were the cords that stretched toward nothing, as if they'd hung on to the family's electronics as long as they could.

"At least they didn't trash the place, I guess." Rob scrubbed a hand through his hair. "Isn't that how it goes in movies?"

"That's when they're searching for intel or stolen treasure." He crossed his arms and tried to suppress a smirk. "Do you have a stash of intel or stolen treasure?"

Rob snorted and shook his head. "Fresh out."

"Good." Stumbling across an international spy ring might've finally proven Cody's worth to his father and landed him that promotion, but it would've also made him late to the retirement party. He checked his watch. Correction: later than he already was. "We'll be in touch."

He stepped out into the winter sunshine. Houses lined both sides of the quiet street. A neighbor peered out from a window across the way, but other officers had already canvassed the area. No witnesses had suspected a problem until squad cars responded to Rob Tropes' call.

A discarded TV box protruded from the recycling bin by the garage. The working theory was that a thief had spotted the box, concluded the family had at least one shiny new gadget, and targeted the house accordingly. With Thanksgiving coming up on Thursday, early Black Friday sales were already in full swing, and homes brimmed with tempting acquisitions. This might be only the first in a string of burglaries.

He'd look for Clara, the community relations officer, at the retirement party and ask her to post on social media, warning residents to keep evidence of their purchases out of plain sight.

Back at the station, a *Congrats* banner sparkled over the breakroom doorway. The thing was wrong on multiple levels. First, nothing about Neenah said glitter was the way to her heart. Second, though the department was celebrating her retirement, the last thing *she* wanted was to be congratulated on the lowlight of her life—being forced to surrender her badge at age thirty-two.

When the usual suspects had volunteered to coordinate this party, Cody let them and focused his energy on cheering up the retiree. He'd mostly failed. Perhaps his time would've been better spent picking décor.

Streamers in primary colors looped along the breakroom ceiling. A big cake featuring Neenah's headshot took up half of a table. Pieces of her were missing, but enough remained to recognize her uniform, something she hadn't worn since the accident back in January.

He scanned the mingling officers and administrative staff, searching for her dark hair. Two brunettes similar to Neenah's height of five-five caught his eye, but he ruled them out. One had curled the ends of her loose hair, and the other wore a uniform over bad posture. The guest of honor wasn't here.

Where would she go to escape her own party?

He passed the ladies' room without slowing. Raised in a household of males, she'd never stow away someplace where the only possible people who'd discover her would be women who'd cluck and coo over her.

Chief Adams focused on his computer, no one in the hot seat across from him, so he hadn't pulled her aside for a final thank you. Not that the man was nearly grateful enough for Neenah's sacrifice.

One of the department's two interview rooms was closed.

Cody stuck his head into the attached observation room. Empty, with the blinds pulled over the window to the interview room. Listening yielded no sounds from inside, but that didn't fool him. He pushed open the door. There she sat—on the table, boots planted on the chair usually occupied by suspects.

At the sight of her, contentment clicked into place. Never mattered the circumstances, proximity to Neenah always had that effect on him. As long as they were together, they could face anything. It was when they were apart that situations got dicey, like that awful day last winter.

For her last day on the force, she'd dressed in all black from boots to sweater. She wore her dark-brown hair in the same low bun she sported most days. Her back remained straight, even as she sat with her hands clasped and her elbows on her knees.

At his entrance, she lifted her face. Shadows underscored her eyes, and a crease marked a line between her brows, but her cheeks weren't red or tear streaked. Her brown eyes scanned him in a practiced glance, then she tipped her face downward again.

He longed for the day when he might guide her to her feet and envelop her in his arms, but she'd set clear boundaries. She wanted him to treat her like he treated Graham, his closest friend behind her. Given how often she'd seen Cody with Graham, she knew they rarely hugged. Maybe once at the guy's wedding, and again when each of Graham's kids were born.

By the time Neenah reached any of those major life milestones, Cody intended to be the man experiencing them with her, not the friend offering a celebratory hug. But for now, he wasn't allowed to say such things.

He swung the door shut behind himself and took a seat on the table facing the opposite direction, his own feet on the chair usually occupied by detectives and officers. "You're missing an awful party out there."

Neenah's laugh was a single, unenthusiastic grunt.

"Did they cut the cake without you, or did you step out after?"

"After."

He waited, but she didn't explain her reasons for leaving. Still, the home break-in was more of a mystery. Neenah was here because, even after the surgeries to replace both her knees and repair the extensive damage, followed by painful rehab and months of light duty, her knees would never allow a return to full duty.

"Who am I supposed to be now?" Her voice was low, which was normal for her, and quiet, which was not.

"Same person you've always been." He swallowed hard. He had more to say, but it wasn't the kind of compliment he'd pay Graham. Yet whether she liked it or not, and no matter who said it or didn't, it was true. She needed to know. "Brave and intelligent Neenah Casper."

She scoffed. "More like unemployed Neenah Casper."

"Who you are goes with you, no matter what your employment status is." He knew how little that would comfort her. Both of them had grown up with police officer fathers. The desire to serve justice and provide safety ran in their blood.

Yet despite his own career goals and his drive to protect the community, if he could go back in time and cover the back of the house instead of approaching the front door, he would. He'd face the impact with the car of fleeing suspects. He'd endure the surgeries and pain and setbacks and early retirement —anything to protect his best friend from this experience, even if the wait for more with her never did come to an end.

"I've never wanted to be anything but a police officer."

Emotion rasped in her voice. "It was all I dreamed about. All I worked for. I loved it. It wasn't supposed to end like this."

"I know."

Neenah made decisions fast and hard. She'd described the childhood pizza nights with her brothers, where she had to take all the food she wanted on the first pass and guard her plate if she didn't want to lose what she had. Changing her mind brought on jeers and unfair trades. "Oh, you want cheese now?" her brothers would ask. "Trade you both your slices of pepperoni for one cheese."

Raised in that environment, Neenah had learned to make firm choices and not to take them back. She'd picked a career and stuck with it in a blaze of passion and pride. And now it'd been ripped away.

"I'm sorry," he said.

She sighed.

"You're going to find a new dream. Some other mission in life."

She issued no audible response.

He didn't blame her. If he lost his place on the force, he'd lose any hope of making his father proud. Neenah probably felt the same way, especially since she had the added pressure of brothers who were also officers, excelling in their roles back in Wyoming, where she grew up.

But there were other options. "I hear the technical college is looking for criminal justice instructors." To position themselves for promotions, he and Neenah had both obtained master's degrees in their off-hours. Though hers wouldn't land her the lieutenant position she'd hoped for anymore, the advanced education did qualify her for an instructor role.

"Those who can't do, teach, huh?" she asked.

"I'm sorry."

Several minutes passed.

"I'm supposed to open gifts in front of everybody."

"Want me to pull the fire alarm?" His father would throw a fit over breaking the law for something as frivolous as someone's feelings, but if forced to choose between his career and Neenah, he'd pull the lever without hesitation.

"If you did that, I'd arrest you myself."

If only she still had that authority.

Her shoes thumped to the ground, and she strode for the door, another decision made and embraced. He followed her brisk return to the breakroom. She circled behind the gift table, and Cody flanked her. Graham took up station on the other side of the table, beside patrol officers Garrett Johnson and Justin McKinnon. If she was going to celebrate forced retirement, she'd do it surrounded by friends.

She lifted the first gift bag like a game show host. "Should we see what you all got me?"

"Oh, that's mine." Burt Quince clapped a handful of popcorn into his mouth. "You're gonna love it."

She eyed the officer as if keeping tabs on a suspect whose vehicle she was about to search for drugs. She removed the tissue paper and peered inside before pulling out prune juice and reading glasses, a smile on her lips and a glare in her eyes. "How thoughtful."

"So you'll be prepared for retirement." Quince grinned and slapped Garrett's shoulder.

Though Garrett was a known jokester, even he shifted away and shook his head with disapproval.

Others, however, laughed. Only the knowledge that she wouldn't want him to step in stopped Cody from pre-screening each item before she got to it. After her double knee replacement, her body might no longer withstand high-impact activities like running, but she was still in the prime of her life. Still courageous, vibrant, beautiful. No one had the right to hint otherwise.

Cody didn't want his own present associated with this

party. He slipped his card off the table. He'd follow her out after the festivities and give it to her by her truck.

"Adams."

Cody wasn't the only Adams at the station, but since that gruff voice belonged to the other one, the summons must've been pointed at him. He turned to find the senior Adams, a stout and barrel-chested man, in the breakroom doorway. Since high school, Cody had called the man *Chief.* Before that, he'd called him *Dad.*

Neenah gave him an encouraging smile that was probably meant to tell him she didn't need him to stay. She went back to her gifts as Chief walked away, too confident Cody would follow to stand around and ensure it. Most of the officers in the department liked Chief Adams. Those who didn't like him at least respected him. Cody included.

But leave Neenah?

She spotted him loitering, and her eyes widened as she pointed after Chief Adams.

He lifted his hands in acquiescence. He'd go, but he was coming right back, even if all he could do once he returned was wait.

* * *

When her parents divorced, Neenah had learned she could do impossibly hard things. First and foremost, she'd survived without her mom in a household of males—half of the time at first, then full-time when her mom's job took her out of state.

But she hadn't survived unscathed. Pieces of her had broken away like a plane turning to shrapnel during a crash landing.

After her mom moved, she'd cried for a month straight, until she realized no one in her house knew how to deal with her tears. Then, she'd toughened up and started looking out for herself.

Circumstances like that changed a person.

Even decades later, she wasn't quite like most other women. She prized career over family and most friendships. Relationships didn't last anyway. Instead of a soft and sweet personality, hers leaned toward assertive and tough. Rather than dreaming about retirement, she'd dreaded it, even before the timetable raced up to meet her here. Today. Another crash landing. What would be left of her when the dust settled this time?

Tears threatened, but she refused to go out on a note of weakness, so she threw herself into putting on a show for her coworkers. After she opened presents, she gathered the discarded gift wrap and tissue paper and dumped it into a garbage can.

"I hope you plan to take some time for yourself." At Jenny's voice, Neenah braced.

Kindness might coax those tears back to the surface. But only if she let it. Proving again that she could do hard things, she smiled at the college intern who worked the front desk.

"I'd say a trip to Hawaii is in order." The curvy redhead inhaled, held her arms out, and turned her face up like she was on a beach enjoying the sun and the aroma of tropical flowers.

A couple of years ago, Neenah wouldn't have turned down a tropical vacation. But now? The fact that she had no job to get back to when it ended would render any trip as dull and gray as one to Ireland without the rolling green hills, castle ruins, and charming accents.

Clara moved in and rubbed a circle on Neenah's shoulder blade. "After everything you've been through, you deserve a break, and you're getting benefits, right? So there's no real rush into the next job?"

Jenny came back from her imaginary vacation, blue eyes widened. "They'd better be taking care of you."

"I'll be fine." Because the accident happened in the line of duty, her medical expenses—and there'd been many—had been covered in full. She'd won a Police Purple Heart and disability retirement benefits. The payments amounted to less than fifty percent of what she'd made while on the force, but the payouts would pad whatever paychecks she earned in the future.

Burt Quince sauntered up. "So what's next for you? Going all in on the retirement thing?"

"I'll find work." She pulsed her jaw, even as she offered the requisite smile. "Would you like the prune juice back? You're closer to retirement age than I am."

"Oh, no, you keep it." He held his hands up as he backed away.

When he was gone again, Clara rolled her eyes. "I can't believe the nerve of some people, acting like a serious injury is something to poke fun at."

"A serious injury is better than the alternative." She easily could've died in the accident.

Seeming to understand the implication, Jenny's eyebrows pinched with concern. Clara frowned.

Neenah's phone buzzed. She needed to get out of there before she let on to how upset she really was, and any excuse would do. Even a spam call. Without checking caller ID, she lifted the device. "Sorry, I have to take this."

She stepped from the breakroom and answered.

"May I speak with Neenah Casper?"

Most spam callers didn't open with her full name. Also, they didn't usually have a mature voice—not old enough for the prune juice, but perhaps old enough for a normal retirement party. She peeked at the display and found an unfamiliar number. "Speaking."

"Neenah, this is Leanne Aldine, Kristi Aldine's mother."

Memories of her best friend in college flashed to mind. In her mid-twenties, fresh off a divorce and with full custody of a young daughter, Kristi had been a non-traditional student pursuing a business degree. She and Neenah met in their gen ed literature class their first semester and hit it off after discovering they'd both been trick riders in high school. Kristi became something of a big sister, and her daughter, Kaylie, like a niece. Together, the pair had offered Neenah something she hadn't experienced since her parents' divorce—a taste of a home with a soft side.

But after graduation, they'd moved in separate directions, Neenah to work in Redemption Ridge, Colorado, and the mother and daughter to another part of Wyoming to help care for Kristi's ailing father. Neenah had reached out, but Kristi rarely replied. When she did, it was only after a week or two delay. They lost touch long before Kristi opened the stationery business she'd dreamed of. Neenah was hurt. Another close relationship, up in flames.

And now, after years of silence, an out-of-the-blue call from Kristi's mom. If her old friend was up for some kind of honor, Neenah wasn't making the trip. Not for someone who couldn't be bothered to call. "What can I do for you?"

"I'm afraid I have bad news." A shudder wove through the words.

Oh. Not an award then.

"What happened?" Neenah asked.

"She had a bad reaction to anesthesia while having her gallbladder removed." Her volume rose like a car hitting an unexpected speed bump. "She died."

Instantly, the hurt surrounding their failed friendship shriveled. Grief hiccupped through Neenah's chest and flushed her cheeks. "I'm so sorry."

Leanne shuddered on the other end of the line.

Neenah dipped her chin, the phone still to her ear, and scrambled for something more to say. "I have some time off. When is the funeral?"

"We—we already had the service. We tried to get the word out. Everything happened so fast. So unexpectedly. We didn't realize someone who needed to know would've been left out."

"It's—" Neenah cleared her throat. "I am truly sorry, but please don't carry any regrets as far as I'm concerned. We haven't spoken in a decade, but I'm so sorry for her and you all." Neenah said a prayer for the girl and was about to ask after her when Leanne dropped her next bomb.

"She named you in her will."

"Named me?" Good thing she had her feet solidly braced, or she'd have stumbled at that revelation. "For what?"

Kristi hadn't been well off while Neenah had known her. She might've built up savings and equity, but surely all of that ought to go to her daughter. However, if she'd started her business after all, she may have wanted an adult to take over. Still, Neenah made a poor choice, because she didn't have—or want—the art, computer, or management skills necessary to run a stationery business.

"She had the will drawn up a couple of years after her divorce, when she was at school and you two were close. I'm not sure she would've gone to the trouble but for Kaylie."

That, at least, made sense, but a low-level hum of foreboding rang in her ears. If this centered around Kaylie and involved Neenah...

"She named you as Kaylie's guardian."

No. She clamped a hand over her mouth to suppress the forceful objection. But really? Kristi knew Neenah's desire to focus on her career, not a family. She used to say Neenah would outgrow her opinion, but it took a lot of nerve to bank a child's future on it. "I'm ... shocked."

"I'm sure she never expected it to come to this," Leanne said. "No one wants to think it might."

Fair enough. Neenah had never expected her life to lead where it had either. "We can contest the will so Kaylie can stay with family. I have zero desire to break you all apart at a time like this."

"Oh, no, dear. Actually, it's, um, an answer to prayer. Kristi is—was—our only child, and her ex, well, good riddance. She had friends, but none so close as you two once were. She was sure you would do right by her baby. She called you the strongest woman she knows."

Flattery couldn't blur the fact that the so-called baby was a teenager, and Neenah's sister-like bond with Kristi had long since faded to memory. "Kaylie would be better off with you. She knows and loves you."

"Harvey has MS. It's progressing, and things are ... difficult. My own health isn't what it once was, either, and I need help keeping up with his needs. We're on a waitlist to move into an assisted living facility in the next couple of months and can't have a teen there."

"Oh. I'm sorry."

"If Kaylie has to go through this, I would much rather she go straight to live with someone who can give her the home she deserves for the next couple of years. And that really is all we're talking about—the next two-and-a-half years, when she'll finish high school." She paused as if to give Neenah a chance to jump on the conversational merry-go-round, but her brain was too dizzy from the first couple of twirls.

Leanne continued. "She's an excellent student—top of her class. Driven. She wants to be a lawyer, and she's the fastest long-distance runner her school has ever had, even though she's only a sophomore. She went to state last month. She is such a good kid, and we want the best life for her. Her mom did too, hence the will and life insurance. There's enough to offset the expenses of Kaylie's care and a fund set aside for her college, so this needn't be a financial burden."

The request sped toward her at one hundred miles per hour. Neenah started walking. Fast. Toward the exit. "Finances are not my primary concern."

Leanne took a shaky inhale. "What is, then, dear?"

She pushed out the doors and onto the steps outside the precinct. Forty-degree air filtered through her sweater and dress pants. She crossed one arm over herself, the phone still clutched to her ear. No one would overhear whatever she said next, but what reason should she give for not taking in the displaced daughter of the best female friend she'd ever had? Kristi was the closest thing she'd had to a sister, if only for a few years.

"I'm not mother material. I know Kristi and I were close once, and maybe she thought I'd settle down one day, but that's not the direction my life has taken. I'm single. Unemployed at the moment. I have no experience raising a child."

"Kaylie has such fond memories of you. You and Kristi took her to a rodeo once? And you won't find a more mature teenager. She just needs a stable adult in her life. Someone who shows up for her by attending her cross-country meets and making sure she gets to school and applies to the right colleges, doesn't go off the deep end with parties and such. You planned to become a police officer, correct? You followed through on that?"

"I did, but I'm ... not anymore. I don't know how I would do this."

"You might surprise yourself, dear, with what you're capable of."

She was most surprised lately by what she *wasn't* capable of. What would Cody, who'd already seen her through so much, say to this? A decision of this magnitude would affect their friendship. Would affect him.

We'll get through this.

How many times had he told her that this year? He was her anchor. Had been for years before the accident and would be no matter what she chose in this situation. If she agreed to this, he'd step up with Kaylie, even if she didn't ask him to, and that thought eased some of the tension binding her chest.

"Kristi kept a picture of you with her and Kaylie on her dresser, and Kaylie has it now. She remembers you. Sometimes, people lose touch without losing love."

Did that count? Wasn't part of love staying in touch? Perhaps, but if so, Neenah had failed at it too. She could've kept reaching out a few more months after the move, waiting for things to settle down. Could've visited.

"That doesn't mean that I'm the right person to step in with her daughter."

"That seems to be everyone's mindset—we asked people we trust whether they could take her in before we found the will. If you're not willing, I'm afraid foster care is a real possibility."

Neenah closed her eyes. Took a deep breath. Foster care could be beautiful. But it could also be terrible. She knew from her work. From her own life, she knew the trauma of divorce, of only hearing from her mother a few times a year. How much worse this situation had to be for Kaylie.

She prayed for guidance. She thought of little Kaylie's giggle, the surge of protectiveness when the girl held her hand in the crowd at the rodeo. Kaylie hadn't needed her then. Kristi had held her other hand. Now, Kaylie had no one else.

As unmoored as Neenah felt, she did have extra time right now. A sense of purpose and certainty took root. God had known how the timing would work out. And through the events of the year, He'd shown her the strength of the support system she had in her church, her friends, and especially Cody.

Her decision solidified.

"What are the next steps?" she asked.

Chapter Two

Cody closed himself in Chief Adams's office and turned to face the man behind the desk. His dad trimmed his light-brown hair every couple of weeks. He kept his uniform crisp, his posture straight, and his face clean-shaven, aside from a mustache he'd had Cody's entire life. Though in his upper fifties, he hadn't eased up on his workouts in the police department's fitness center before every shift.

Chief interlaced his fingers. "Sloane's decided to retire."

Detective Sloane was one of the older guys. Rumor had it, he'd stayed on as long as he had at Chief's request, as if Cody and others weren't eager for the opportunity to move up. The decision had irked him, but Chief speaking with Cody now that the time had come showed unusual favor. Technically, decisions about his employment were supposed to fall to others, but no one got ahead without Chief's approval. He must've claimed the task of announcing Cody's promotion to him personally.

Accomplishment swelled in his chest.

Earning his father's respect had been a lifelong endeavor,

one rewarded only by a gleam of pride when Cody first announced his intention to become a cop and again when he'd been sworn in. Finally, this time, he'd hear a *well done*. To think, this morning when he'd resisted cutting corners, he might've done himself a favor, not some other detective. He silently thanked God.

Chief's lips tightened. No wonder. Offering congratulations must be like a foreign language to him. "You and Quince are in the running to take Sloane's place."

Satisfaction drained from him, leaving him hollow, a uniform floating on a ghost. This wasn't a promotion; it was a competition, and against Burt Quince of all people. Did his father truly consider them equals?

Chief barreled on. "As things are being decided, you'll each be assigned some investigations. Do well, and the promotion could be yours, but don't expect any favoritism."

"Of course not." The ghost had a voice. A gruff one.

"Quince is motivated. He's wanted this, and he has seniority. Don't underestimate him."

Sensation returned, a bruising blow to his chest as if his body armor had taken a bullet. "Understood."

Chief exhaled long and slow, his pale-blue eyes assessing him.

He knew the look well. He waited to hear what technicality branded him a failure in his father's opinion this time.

"If you're distracted, this won't go well for you."

"Distracted?"

"Her job might be changing, but my concerns have not."

The only possible "her" was Neenah. Chief discouraged his officers from dating each other. Though no formal policy forbade it, provided the couple wasn't in each other's chain of command, Chief believed romantic ties undercut the integrity of the force.

"After today, she won't be a police officer anymore," Cody returned.

"Not in title, but mark my words, she'll want to be as involved as possible, and with someone as impulsive as she is, that's a recipe for disaster. It's a wonder her rash decisions took as long as they did to catch up with her. I won't stand for her pulling you down with her."

The heat in his chest morphed from pain to anger. Neenah's gutsy choices had raised a few eyebrows, but she'd never strayed far enough from policy to warrant a formal reprimand. The only people who seemed to mind were Cody, who preferred her to err on the safe side, and Chief, who seemed to have extended his fault-finding mission from Cody to Neenah. A consequence of being Cody's friend, he suspected.

"There was nothing impulsive about her actions on the day of her accident."

"Regardless, she needs a clean break from all this." He waved a hand.

Was Cody supposed to be included in that clean break? Didn't matter. He wasn't giving her up. She couldn't have a clean break after all that had happened anyway. Her injuries and recovery had been messy. The fact that he was competing for a promotion as she left was messy. Thinking about her in some other job without him there to watch her back and she his? Messy.

"Something's kept you stagnant." His father's glare raked him. "You could've made detective when Lockhart did."

"Instead of him, you mean?"

Chief shrugged.

Graham Lockhart had been Cody's best friend until Graham went and fell in love. They were still close, but these days, Cody saw a lot more of Neenah because Graham had a young family to dote on. He'd needed the better hours and pay that came with the investigator role, and Cody wouldn't have tried to take that away. "Graham is a top-notch investigator."

"And you wouldn't have been?" Chief lifted an eyebrow.

"We're about to see, aren't we?" Cody clenched his jaw. "What cases am I working on?"

"Start with the home burglary."

"Yes, sir. Anything else?"

"That's all."

Cody let himself out, but instead of starting the investigation, he searched for Neenah. She'd left her own party, and the few still eating cake didn't know where she'd gone. He slogged through the rest of his shift and then headed to her house.

Her one-story home stood on a few acres at the edge of town. A small barn and paddock out back housed her horse. A couple of strings of Christmas lights hugged her porch railing, even though Thanksgiving was still a few days off.

He rang the bell and tapped the card he'd gotten her against his hand.

Snow-capped mountains jutted into the sky, but around him golden grass and sage covered the land, punctuated by the occasional house or stand of pines. A whinny rose, and cattle grazed in the distance.

He pushed the button again.

Footsteps sounded on the other side of the door, and finally, it swung open.

Neenah had swapped her neat bun for a ponytail and changed into a T-shirt and leggings. Hard to imagine those shapely legs were the cause of her retirement. "What's up?" she asked.

He wrenched his focus to her face. On the way, he noted she rested her hands on her hips, and her breath came a little quick.

"Working out?"

"No. Just ..." She pointed farther inside, then waved as if

to say *never mind*. Her eyes sharpened on the envelope. "What brings you by?"

The gift. The news of his potential promotion. Concern for her. Hope—frail as it was—for their future. "Wanted to make sure you're all right."

She gave a lackluster smile and padded into the house.

He followed her to the guest bedroom she used as a catch-all space. Boxes, exercise equipment, kitchen appliances, and a few power tools lay scattered across the floor, blocking the way to the twin bed and the cluttered desk. At least, at first glance. Neenah picked her way through the chaos like a cat stalking through an obstacle course.

"Bomb squad didn't arrive in time?" he asked.

She snorted. "I'm reorganizing." She plucked a stack of paperwork from the desk, flipped through it, and tucked it into a file folder. Given the day she'd had, he expected the humor to fade, but she shot him another smile and shook her head, apparently still enjoying the joke. "Sometimes things have to get worse before they get better."

"I see." With that mindset, maybe he should rip the bandage off and tell her about the detective opening. Instead of feeling left behind, she might be happy for him. But then he imagined her getting even quieter, closing him out, losing touch. He couldn't allow things to get any worse. They needed to skip straight to better.

He scanned the mess. To be knee-deep in cleaning out her spare room, she must've started as soon as her shift ended. Moving at this pace, she'd have her whole house and barn renovated before the year's end in just over a month. "How can I help?"

"I'm donating everything in that pile." With a pointed finger, she circled a stack of boxes and garbage bags that stood as high as his shoulder.

"I'll load it in my truck."

"No, mine. I'll have time to take it tomorrow morning. Since I don't have a job and all."

As if she'd been fired.

"Things have to get worse before they get better, right?" he asked.

She grunted.

He set the card on the floor in the hall, slung two bags off the top of the pile, and carried them to his own truck. Back inside, he stashed the card on the kitchen counter for later. He returned to the guest room and lifted an edge of the next box on the pile to judge its weight.

"What did Chief Adams want?"

Feigning concentration, he shifted the next box down, even though he'd already decided the top box alone would strain the handles punched into the sides of the cardboard.

"Cody?"

He was much better at ferreting out the truth than hiding it, and where Neenah was concerned, he was already hiding too much—feelings for her that never had obeyed her order to stick to the friend zone. He lifted the top box and spit out the less dangerous truth. "Detective Sloane is retiring. Chief wants me and Quince helping with investigations."

Without giving her a chance to reply, he ducked out.

She would know being tapped to help equated to an audition of sorts.

Empty-handed, he headed back in.

Neenah had a fist propped against her hip and fire in her eyes. "I can't believe your own father is making you compete against Burt Quince. He must know who the better man is."

She thought he was the better man? Before his smile could break free, his father's warnings about Quince replayed in his mind. "Chief's never been all that impressed with me."

Neenah studied him, then turned away and retrieved a

shoebox from the upper closet shelf. "I think it's the opposite."

"Sure. That's why he never made it to my high school football games. And why, when I joined the force, he assigned me to the worst training officer he had. And why, today, he thought I needed to be reminded to not get distracted from my job."

She opened the lid on the box and picked through the contents. "He told me himself he plans for you to follow in his footsteps all the way to the top."

The idea spooked an unexpected laugh from his chest. "What?"

She shrugged. "He expects you to be chief one day."

The man who'd never once expressed pride in his son? Cody's imagination sputtered and died, unable to conjure a picture of the man admitting he'd one day retire, let alone pass the reins to him. "When was this?"

"A few years ago."

That made even less sense. She'd never breathed a word about this before. What reason could she have to keep it a secret? Not to mention that to be on track for chief of police, he should've been promoted years ago.

Neenah replaced the cover on the box and slid it onto one of her piles. "Anyway, you have to beat Quince out for the job."

"You sure you want me to?"

She straightened, eyes brimming with curiosity. "Why wouldn't I?"

He crossed his arms. The chasm of things they didn't discuss was bigger than he'd known if she'd kept a personal conversation with Chief secret. Maybe he shouldn't outright ask if it bothered her that he was up for a promotion the same day she'd been retired.

"You think I'm jealous?" She averted her gaze. "The

world's going to keep spinning. Besides ..." She offered a fleeting smile. "I want good things for you, regardless of my career prospects."

He believed her, yet her movements grew slow and heavy. She was sad to be on the outside of the police force, and as a part of the department, he could only offer so much comfort. He resigned himself to the task she'd offered him, and soon the pile from the bedroom filled the bed of his truck.

Meanwhile, Neenah finished with the desk and closet and pointed him toward a box with a food processor, a toaster, and a couple of other small appliances. "I think there's space for them on the kitchen counter."

He snagged the box, only then realizing she'd saved the heavier item, a stand mixer made of thick metal, for herself. With her usual energy, she led the way to the kitchen and hefted the mixer onto the counter. The prominent placement made no sense for someone who'd never been a cook or a baker.

"You sure you want all this out?" he asked. "The top cabinet shelves would keep them out of your way."

She eyed the cabinet doors the way one might assess storm clouds.

"I know for a fact they're empty," he said.

"I don't like to store things where I can't reach them."

"That's a limiting way to live when you're only five-five." A height he knew by feel when it came to Neenah because, yeah, maybe he'd paid a little too much attention to how they fit together the few times they'd embraced. His body had stored away the memory of the precious weight of her head against his chest, the feminine scent of her hair wafting up to his nose.

She rolled her eyes, which were at the level of his collarbone.

Staying in the friend zone might be easier if he quit cataloging every fact about her as it related to him.

He opened one of the cabinets and assessed the top shelf. It was tall enough to hold the toaster and the food processor. The stand mixer might require them to lower the shelf a few inches. "All this time, you've preferred to walk to the spare room to get this stuff instead of using a stool?"

"It hasn't been a problem. I don't really use these things."

He turned from the cabinet. "Then why put them on the counter where you have to look at them every day?"

"Someone might use them someday."

"Who? What day?"

She crossed her arms and shrugged. This was one of her fast and stubborn decisions. One she probably regretted already, but she was too committed to take it back on her own.

He chuckled. "Do you *have* a step stool?"

"In the closet." She hiked a thumb toward the hall they'd just walked.

He found a folding two-step ladder stuffed beside the vacuum and returned to the kitchen as he popped it open. "If you kept it closer, you might not mind using it so much."

Neenah leaned against the far counter.

He stepped up to assess the situation. The glasses on the shelf below were short enough for him to lower the top shelf and fit the mixer in. Holes extended down the inside of the prefab cabinets. He only needed to move the pegs supporting the shelf. "I can't believe you have all this space and you're not using it because you're too proud to use a step stool."

"Says the guy who doesn't want anyone to see him use a mounting block to get on a horse."

She had him there. But to his credit, she had to live with the arrangement of her house every day while he only went riding once or twice a year with their friends. And even that was merely to spend all the time with Neenah that he could.

The sound of paper tearing stopped his train of thought. Holding the half-lowered shelf so it didn't crush her glassware, he peered over his shoulder.

Neenah pulled his card from the envelope. For a guy who was supposed to be nothing more than a friend, he'd spent way too long trying to choose the right one. The cards he'd watched her open at the party today were either retirement jokes or upbeat and congratulatory. His was not. He'd found it in the sympathy section under a tab labeled *Support—Friend*.

It contained more heartfelt sentiments than a man could share with a female friend he didn't have feelings for. Would Neenah recognize that? The verdict took forever as her eyes ticked over each line of text. Next time, he would pick one with two sentences, tops.

He returned to his task and lowered the other pegs, then lifted in the appliances.

"Thank you." Her voice, always soothingly low, rasped with emotion.

He climbed off the step stool and tugged the hem of his shirt straight. "You're welcome."

She lifted the certificate. "This is thoughtful."

He dipped his chin. The paper represented a one-year prepaid membership to a gym in town, since Neenah could no longer use the fitness center in the station. "I got one for myself too."

She frowned. "You didn't have to do that."

"This situation is bad enough. I'm not giving up my workout partner."

Lips still downturned, she looked away with a shaky sigh. "Everything's different."

"Not everything." He was still around.

Tears welled in her eyes.

The uncharacteristic show of emotion meant he got to offer uncharacteristic care.

"Come here." He opened his arms, and she stepped into them. "Sometimes things get worse before they get better, but they *are* going to get better." He would make sure of it.

She snuggled against his chest. Right where she belonged.

Could she feel in the way he held her that he'd do anything to help her rebuild a life she loved? She lifted her face, and her gaze rested on his mouth, not his eyes. The brown of her irises seemed to darken with intent, like maybe she felt the same things he did. Like maybe she was about to act on years of latent attraction that hadn't been as one-sided as he'd feared.

But then she turned her face to the side and said, "I'm taking in a kid."

* * *

During the hours they'd spent working out together, Neenah had watched Cody maintain peak physical fitness. In her weaker moments, she'd sneaked peeks at him in the gym mirrors the way some women sneaked chocolate. The man had earned the firm muscle tone she felt in the contours of his body as they embraced.

The warm weight of his arms cradled her against the knit of his long-sleeve shirt. She could tell he lowered his head toward her, because his breath caressed her forehead.

Lulled into a comfortable haze, she lifted her face toward his. Her lips tingled as if she weren't just imagining the textures of his skin and mouth. If she closed the gap, he'd get over his surprise pretty quickly. He'd claim her lips in a kiss that—

No. She wasn't allowing a kiss, even in her imagination.

So, she looked away and said the one thing she knew would change the trajectory of the moment. "I'm taking in a kid."

Under her hands, his back tensed. His abs tightened too,

and the rise and fall of his chest hitched. She shouldn't stay latched onto him like a human lie detector reading his every reaction. She shifted away.

He rolled his shoulders like he did before picking up a one-hundred-pound barbell. "What kid?"

She explained. As she ended with the few facts she knew about Kaylie, her stomach churned with discomfort. "In retrospect, I shouldn't have taken her grandmother's word for it. I haven't known Kaylie since kindergarten. I might be inviting a rebellious teenager into my house for the next two-and-a-half years. Or longer. Lots of kids don't leave home once and for all at eighteen. College might not work out. Or maybe she'll need a place to come back to over summers, and if she doesn't get a job right away—"

He raised a hand, and she fell silent. He stayed frozen for a beat. "Let's not borrow trouble."

Right. Each day had enough of that for itself.

This was the kind of calm assurance she'd needed, but what did it cost him? What was going on in his head right now?

"This is why we needed to clean out the guest room?" he asked.

We. Wherever his thoughts were racing, he'd connected himself with her in that simple word. For a woman who wasn't interested in dating, that companionship brought too much comfort. "Technically, I was getting the room ready by myself."

He lifted an eyebrow as if to ask if she really thought he'd let her work alone. "When is she coming?"

"I'm flying out tomorrow, and we're going to drive Kristi's SUV, loaded with Kaylie's things, back Friday or Saturday."

"You leave tomorrow?"

She nodded. This was all happening suddenly, but Kaylie needed a home.

"And you weren't going to tell me?"

"I did. I am. *I* just found out a couple of hours ago." She ran a hand over her mouth to stop the excuses. The truth was, she hadn't wanted to tell him. But why? The man was her best friend. When he added the benefit of his quiet strength to whatever impulsive decisions she made, they became unstoppable.

She gulped. "This wasn't part of my plan. I'm doing it, but it's scary. It's scary even to talk about. I'm still dazed that I'm not a cop anymore. And now I'm about to be someone's guardian. By not mentioning it, for a little longer, we got to be Cody and Neenah the way we've always been, instead of Cody and Neenah and this thing she said she'd never do."

"Help an orphan? I don't recall banning that in our Bill of Friendship." His mouth twitched as if he thought that was clever. "You taking in a kid who needs you would be a weird thing for me to take offense at."

"I once told you my life isn't about ... family."

Cody's eyes narrowed. "I believe the exact quote was ..." He cleared his throat and lifted the pitch of his voice a few notes. "'My life isn't about *romance* and family. I'm focused on my career.'"

Heat radiated from her cheeks. He remembered word-for-word what she'd answered when he'd asked her out. Embarrassment could sear a moment into memory, but Cody was a blond whose skin flushed if he was embarrassed or angry, and no extra color shaded his cheeks.

So what was this?

Had he repeated her words to get a read on her feelings? He might still be interested. If she had, say, kissed him, would he have kissed her back?

Excitement swooped through her stomach, and she pressed a hand against it. She could be reading too much into this, and even if not, she wanted normal. She wanted her plans back. Dating her best friend was not on her retirement bucket list. If she was thinking about Cody in romantic terms, she hadn't just lost her job. She'd lost her mind.

His voice remained calm and steady. "Given you're between careers, it's logical you'd focus on something else."

Something else like a romance with him? She opened her mouth. Closed it.

"Kaylie?" he prompted. "That's her name, right?"

Ah. "Yes."

He'd moved on from talk of a potential relationship faster than she had. Of course he wouldn't still harbor feelings for her after all this time, when she had so little to offer. When she'd been more of a burden than anything else for almost a year.

She stilled her fidgety hands. "My job situation makes it possible to take her, and I think it's the right thing to do. But for the record, I'm not *actually* retired. I will be getting another job. I have to."

He nodded slowly. "Because you planned to."

"Yes, that and my benefits aren't one hundred percent. Besides, what's so wrong with plans?"

His smile pulled to one side. "What's wrong with adventure?"

"Adventures like this year mean a lot of loss." She'd already lost her job. If she and Cody attempted a romance and came up short of happily ever after, the loss of their friendship would hurt worse than the loss of her real, flesh-and-bone knees. Before she could wallow, she pulled her shoulders back. "Anyway, I need income, and I'd be bored out of my mind without work."

"Even with Kaylie?"

"Of course. She's a high schooler, so she won't need or want constant attention."

"She did just lose her mom. That's bound to add some complications."

The statement served as a warning light. She might have time, but her other qualifications didn't much apply to a grieving teen. "Hopefully not full-time complications."

"Hopefully." He pointed toward the spare room. Kaylie's room. "You want some more help getting that place in shape? If you're leaving tomorrow, you don't have much time."

She sighed. He'd already done more than enough, but he was right, and Kaylie would need a space of her own to retreat into when she got here.

So, as she feared, they became Cody and Neenah and at least one thing—but maybe two—she said she'd never do.

Chapter Three

Cody sat at his computer, but his mind refused to focus on the details about the burglary on the screen before him. Instead, though it'd been days already, his thoughts kept wandering back to Neenah's kitchen. To that hug. To the way she'd peered up at him—or, more accurately, at his mouth.

Neenah wanted to make a move. He was almost certain.

Why hadn't she?

Was he really that good at hiding what he felt, or was she that unobservant?

He ruled out both possibilities. Most of their friends had, at one point or another, in one way or another, let him know they'd caught on to his feelings for her. And Neenah was a good cop. Observation was her bread and butter. Right up there with the courage to take action.

Changing her mind, however, went against her nature. He'd talked her into using the cabinet's top shelf easily, but that decision had been newer and less important than her longstanding decision to stay squarely in the friend zone. Convincing her to let their friendship advance into a romance would require a skill set even the best hostage negotiator on the force didn't have. Unless he wanted to risk the closest relationship he had, he couldn't begin the conversation until he confirmed more than a fleeting fancy drove that moment in the kitchen.

After all, she'd assured him the last time he'd asked her out that if he ever did so again, their friendship would be over.

Her trip to collect Kaylie bought him some time to consider his options. Since leaving, she'd only texted a handful of times. Sounded like she had her hands full, making arrangements and packing. While he'd spent most of yesterday, Thanksgiving, at Piper and Graham's house, eating and watching football, she'd barely had time to sample the turkey breast and sweet potatoes Kaylie's grandma roasted.

A shape moved beyond his computer as a coworker approached. Graham set a coffee in an open space by the keyboard. "How's it going, Detective?"

Cody grunted. "I'm not a detective yet."

"A technicality. Your time's coming." Graham rolled a chair up to Cody's desk, then leaned heavily against the armrest to eye the photograph on the screen, captured at the latest scene. The homeowners had placed the box for the new TV in the recycling bin, but they'd failed to break it down to fit inside. The protruding image of a flatscreen could've served as a billboard inviting a thief to drop in when the owner pulled out.

"I take it the social media post about properly disposing of electronics boxes wasn't effective," Graham said. "Think it's the same guy?"

"That's the theory." Cody clicked ahead to the next photo. "The back door was forced, like at the last house. This one had a doorbell cam, but only on the front. The intruder reached out—wearing gloves—and covered it with tape from the inside, presumably so he could pull into the driveway to load up his vehicle. No one saw anything."

"Any helpful footage from across the street?"

"Not directly. Small town. It's hard enough convincing a few people here and there to lock their doors. Even fewer bother with doorbell cams."

Graham shifted his foot back and forth, swiveling his chair. "Lab get anything back to you yet from the first crime scene?"

"No. I'll be lucky to get results before this guy cleans out another dozen houses."

Graham tipped his head in acknowledgement. "Both burglaries occurred in the same neighborhood. We'll increase patrols. People will be more vigilant."

"If it results in a new lead, I'll take it. Quince already caught the kid who went for a joyride in Chester Roarke's sports car."

Graham scoffed. "Jasper could've caught him."

"For a four-year-old, your son is pretty quick in that plastic car of his." The toy had been a gift from Cody and Neenah.

"I swear"—Graham lifted a hand—"he's looking forward to opening whatever you two get him this year more than what Piper and I put under the tree."

Before Cody could gloat, his phone buzzed. He scooped it up.

Just a spam text.

"Expecting to hear from someone?" Graham asked.

"Neenah ..." Had almost kissed him. And he wasn't going to be the one to almost kiss and tell. "... is off picking up Kaylie. I'm waiting to hear how things are going."

"You're worried?"

"She was going through a lot, even before taking in a grieving teenager."

"Maybe it'll be good. Give her something meaningful to do."

Maybe. But she'd almost kissed him. And it was the girl she mentioned to break the moment.

"You know ..." Graham tapped his fingers on his armrest. "Without the job to keep her busy, maybe she won't be so career-minded anymore."

Cody pressed his mouth shut. That had occurred to him, of course. And maybe to Neenah too. Maybe that was why she'd had that moment of weakness. Nonetheless, she'd limited it to a moment. "She plans to find something else."

"Her next job might not be as all-consuming as her dedication to the force. She could have bandwidth for other things—and I don't just mean Kaylie."

He meant Cody. Love. A family.

Allowing hopes like those to soar too high could crush him if they plummeted into disappointment. "Only time will tell."

His phone vibrated again, this time with a call. Though Neenah's name wasn't on the display, there wasn't much else to say to Graham, so Cody answered. "Hey, Garrett, what've you got?"

"Another theft over on Eighth Street," the officer said. "You want to come check it out?"

"On my way."

But as he left Graham behind and listened to the description of the crime, his hope of catching a break in his burglary case ebbed. Standing at the scene fifteen minutes later, the situation read like a prank. If not for the homeowner's convincing disappointment, he might even suspect his coworkers of hazing him.

"Last night, they were all standing right here." Carl Dobbs swept his hands through the air as if to direct an airplane to land on top of the pile of coal ten inches from his feet. "And now the whole family's gone without a trace."

Not exactly. The unusual prints and the coal were traces. They simply weren't helpful. A couple of stores in town sold coal to people who used it for heating. As for the footprints, Cody eyed the closest one. Twice the size of his own foot, the prints appeared to belong to an overgrown bear. The depth of the print could provide some information about the size of the foot inside, but they'd need more than that to find the culprit.

Carl scratched his head, displacing his knit cap. "They say there've been a few thefts around town lately. I just don't get why somebody would want our nativity set. We like it, but it's been bleached by the sun over the years. You think they've got a beef with Jesus? One of those types who wants to take Christ out of Christmas?"

Cody eyed the officer who'd been first on scene. Garrett appeared to be holding in laughter. Couldn't blame the guy, but Carl had been upset enough to call the police.

Cody fought to remain serious. "Hard to say what the motive is. Did they take—or leave—anything else?"

"No, sir. Just the Holy Family is gone, and coal and prints appeared in their place."

Spacious yards stretched between the homes and the street. Even if neighbors had security cameras, they likely wouldn't trigger for activity all the way over here. If they did, the footage would be blurry at best. "Do you have any cameras that might have captured a visual?"

"No. Not real worried about crime. We're big on shopping local, so we don't have much that might get stolen off our porch."

About the only similarity between this and the burglaries was the extension cord that still snaked across the lawn to where the light-up family had once gathered. Cody asked Garrett to check in with the neighbors, then turned back to the homeowner. "You have any idea why someone might leave coal for you? Anyone who might have a grudge?"

"No. We ..." His lips dipped in a thoughtful frown, and he shook his head. "We haven't had any run-ins with anybody. We're retired. We spend time with the grands. I putter around the yard. Mina is active on her committees. I suppose it's possible there was some kind of dispute on one of those, but I can't imagine anyone who's active in the church or the community resorting to this kind of behavior to solve a conflict."

"Mina is your wife, Wilhelmina Dobbs?"

Carl nodded. "She's out Black Friday shopping with our daughter. You don't think she crossed paths with someone today who would come here for revenge? Another shopper?"

"At this juncture, I think the most likely theory is it's a prank. Someone thought leaving coal and these footprints would be funny." And hopefully that someone wasn't Garrett or another of Cody's friends. His buddy Gideon Reynolds had once taken out a billboard ad to find a wife for his brother Zeke Reynolds—without Zeke's knowledge. Meanwhile, Will Price didn't always consider the consequences of his actions, or he wouldn't have landed the family ranch in serious financial trouble a couple of years ago. And fun-loving Clint Taylor could probably justify a stunt like this if he had in mind to return the decorations soon, no worse for wear. Carting off a nativity set, leaving coal, and putting Garrett up to calling Cody would hardly qualify as an elaborate scheme for any of them. And if they'd all put their heads together, look out.

Cody offered his business card to Carl. "We'll see if the neighbors can provide any insight, and we'll keep an eye out in case the set turns up. If your wife has any additional thoughts when she gets home, have her give me a call. Or if you think of anything else."

"Will do." Carl opened his wallet and slipped the card inside.

Cody met up with Garrett by the squad cars.

The other officer flashed his notepad, where he'd made a few scribbles. "Got nothing from the neighbors."

"And no other information from other sources?"

Garrett cocked his head. "What other sources?"

"Any of the guys. Or your own sense of humor."

Garrett snickered. "Nope. Chief would not take kindly to an officer being an accomplice to a theft. Besides, I feel kind of bad for Carl. He seems to care a lot about his nativity. If this is a prank, it's not one of mine. No one's said anything to me."

"Has anyone *written* anything to you? Or *done* something suspicious?"

"Come on, man." Garrett slugged his shoulder. "None of the above. I want you to get the job. I wouldn't waste your time. I don't know anything more than you do."

"Okay." He nodded once and winced. "Sorry I asked."

Garrett tucked away his notepad. "Don't go that far. The day you stop asking questions like that is the day we get you good." He gave a jaunty salute and hopped in his car.

Cody got behind the wheel, but before pulling away from the curb, the location app on his phone drew him to click. A map appeared, and he clicked on his favorite contact to pull up her location. The screen reloaded, and the marker showing Neenah's location flashed along a highway a few hours away.

Neenah was on her way back to Redemption Ridge.

* * *

Neenah texted Cody while she waited outside the gas station bathroom for Kaylie.

NEENAH

Nearing the Colorado state line. Be home in
a few hours.

CODY

How is it going? You two hit it off?

She drummed her fingertips against her phone case, replaying the strange couple of days. Kaylie had hung back when Neenah arrived at the airport but warmed up by the time they reached her grandmother's house.

NEENAH

She inherited her mom's enthusiasm for
new things. Most of the time, it's impossible
to tell how sad she has to be.

CODY

Probably still in shock. Give her time.

Good advice, but what then? After the shock, Kaylie would take an emotional nosedive, wouldn't she? And how could Neenah help with that?

The bathroom door swung open, and Kaylie stepped out. The teenager had inherited Kristi's sandy-brown hair, full face shape, and slim build. Her lips were fuller and her nose wider than her mother's had been, but her sunny attitude was also all Kristi. On seeing Neenah, her eyebrows squiggled in question.

Okay, waiting right outside the restroom might fall in the overcautious category, but she'd witnessed society's bad side, and forced retirement didn't erase those memories. She refused to risk the teen getting nabbed from a gas station within the first few hours of Neenah's guardianship. Instead of explaining, she slid her phone away and accompanied her into the crowded aisles.

"Oh!" Kaylie hopped to the nearest display and picked up

a double pack of coconut-covered snack cakes. She wiggled the snack and flashed a toothy grin. "Can we?"

"You can." Neenah lifted a bag of bacon-and-cheddar potato chips. "These are more my speed."

Her golden-brown eyes glowed with the joy of having a junk food accomplice. "Drinks too?"

"What's a road trip without them?" Neenah motioned her to lead the way, curious whether she'd go for coffee or soft drinks.

Instead, Kaylie claimed a juice smoothie.

"Good idea." Neenah chose one for herself. The more natural option wouldn't leave her feeling as wired and trapped in the car for the next five hours.

After Neenah paid for their purchases, they returned to Kristi's SUV. Kaylie's SUV, now, except Kaylie had her learner's permit, not a full license.

Neenah started the ignition, but then looked over at her charge. "You sure you don't want to drive for an hour or so?"

"Aren't we just about out of Wyoming? My permit's only good in the state that issued it, isn't it?"

Neenah shook her head. Even months of desk duty didn't erase her years of experience enforcing traffic laws. "Colorado allows out-of-state learner's permits as long as you have someone twenty-one or older with you. Which I am. Obviously. So you can drive."

Kaylie scrunched her nose and took a swig of her juice.

"You've had your permit for months, right? Your grandma said you've been practicing?"

"Yeah, but just in town. The one time a cop was behind me, I started sweating *so* bad."

Neenah's eyes flicked to the rearview mirror on instinct, though she hadn't pulled out of the parking spot yet. They'd packed the back of the vehicle with Kaylie's things, but they'd left the top open so the mirror still reflected the view. "I don't see any officers now."

Kaylie dipped her chin and blinked at her.

"I'm not on the force anymore. Even if I were, the police aren't the enemy. Their job is to ensure everyone's safety. If you follow the law, you have nothing to worry about."

Kaylie pursed her lips as if to say, "If you say so." Then she lifted her drink and took a long sip.

"I'm also your only option for getting practice in."

She fit the lid back on her drink. "It's just kind of different, you know?"

Wasn't that the truth?

Everything was different. "We'll ease into it." As much as the situation allowed anyway.

Neenah steered toward the interstate. They wouldn't be on it long. Most of this trip would be on state highways, winding south through mountains, valleys, and plains until they reached Redemption Ridge in Colorado's Western Slope. "Good news is, Colorado's driving age is sixteen, not sixteen-and-a-half like Wyoming. As long as we can meet the other requirements, you could have your license six months earlier."

"I haven't taken driver's ed yet."

"In Redemption Ridge, you can take that at school. Once your transfer is approved, we'll see if we can get you enrolled in driver's ed next semester." That step would be simple compared to all the paperwork Kaylie's grandmother had tackled in the last few days on their behalf.

"What's the high school like?"

Neenah pulled into the passing lane to get around a slow-moving truck. "I think it's about the same size as what you're used to. Bryce seems to like it okay."

"Who's Bryce?"

"He's my friend's nephew." He had lived with his aunt, Piper, until earlier in the year when his dad finished his sentence for drug-related charges. Thankfully, both father and son were doing well now, and Bryce was one of the few high school students Neenah had regular contact with through her friends. "He's a junior. I'm sure you'll see him around."

"Is he cute?"

"He's sixteen."

"Would *I* think he was cute?"

"Maybe." His boyish round cheeks had thinned some with age, and he currently towered a good six inches taller than Neenah. She couldn't get on board with his hairstyle or clothes, but teen styles had been less and less understandable the further she got into her thirties.

She was partial to clean-cut men in uniform. Emphasis on the word *men*. And really, her partiality only extended to one off-limits man.

"I'll let you judge for yourself. My friends get together pretty often, and Bryce and his dad come regularly. That is, if you want to come too. Otherwise, you can do your own thing."

"I don't have my own thing."

"Then my things will be your things, at least until you're back in school and have plans of your own."

"Tell me about your friends?" Thin hope lifted Kaylie's voice.

Understandable. An adult's friends would make a poor substitute for peers of her own.

Cody came to mind first. Cody, the man she'd almost kissed. The man she'd been missing constantly. The man she couldn't fall for. If they dated and broke up, she'd be lost without him, especially now that she could use his help with Kaylie. She couldn't risk everything over a little what-if.

She started with her other friends.

"Piper is Bryce's aunt. She owns a consignment and resale shop and is married to Graham Lockhart, a detective. They have two kids. Through them, I got to know Hollis and Lucy Price. Do you follow rodeo at all?"

She shrugged one shoulder. "I'm more into running."

"Fair enough. Hollis is pretty well known. He took a break for a few years, but he and his brother, Will, who you'll also see around, qualified for nationals in team roping. When they're not competing in rodeos, Hollis and Will run their family's quarter horse ranch. That's where my horse, BeeBee, is while I'm gone. Hollis's wife, Lucy, is a veterinarian. She's pregnant with their first." She glanced over in time to see Kaylie nod, but if the girl remembered all these details, Neenah would be impressed. After the deluge of information, she could slip in the name of the last member of her primary friend group without raising questions. "Last, there's Cody Adams. He's a police officer, which I know is your favorite."

"Is *he* cute?"

A flare shot through her chest. She covered with a laugh. "What a question to ask."

Kaylie shrugged. "There was something about how you said his name."

"How was it different from the way I said Will's name? He's single too. Anyway, both of them are way too old for you."

"I'm not the only one in the car."

Neenah scoffed despite the fire raging across her cheeks. Cody wasn't cute. He was handsome. He kept his hair short and neat. Intelligence marked his blue eyes. His face was square and strong. And he made the uniform look good.

A quiet laugh from the passenger seat snapped her back to the conversation. "Sounds like a yes."

Her grip on the steering wheel tightened. What was she supposed to do? Admit her feelings for her best friend to a fifteen-year-old? She'd barely admitted them to herself, let alone to another soul.

GPS instructed her to turn off the interstate and pick up the state highway that would carry them into Colorado. As though the directions took all her focus, she silently found her way.

Once they were settled on the road again, she felt Kaylie's attention on her.

"I'm not dating anyone—and I'm not interested in changing that." Two truths she could hide her crush behind.

"Why not? My mom said no dating until I'm sixteen. I can't wait."

Great. In a matter of months she'd have a dating teenager on her hands. Heaven help her. She tried to find comfort in the fact that Kaylie had admitted her mom wanted her to wait, even though she could've said anything.

"It sounds fun," Kaylie prodded. "So why not?"

"Because I don't plan to get married, and I'm not going to lead anyone on."

"Why don't you want to get married?"

Wasn't the *why* phase supposed to happen long before age fifteen? "I've been fulfilled by my job and faith and friends. I know it's not common, but I'm perfectly content being single. The last time I dated someone was nothing but ... an extra that wasn't all that fun. God made me to be single."

"What wasn't fun about it?"

If this kept up much longer, she would outlaw any more questions until after they reached their destination. "He didn't like my job—thought it was too dangerous and unlady-like. He thought when we got married, I should quit and raise kids. But I've never been very good at being ladylike."

"But you said Cody's a cop. He can't mind your job."

"Right. While I had it." Unfortunately, his father—their boss's boss—hadn't liked her much as a cop and even less as a potential match with his son. But even if she'd been willing to risk Chief Adam's disapproval, another obstacle remained.

"Even Cody wants a family. We've been friends long enough for me to know that. I'm not mother material."

Her passenger didn't reply.

Oh, what was she saying? She couldn't talk about her inability to mother a child with a girl who now depended on her.

She hoped her smile offered reassurance. "I don't think either of us want me to try to replace your mom."

Kaylie nodded, though grief lurked in her eyes.

Neenah fixed her gaze back on the road. "Let's think of me more as your aunt. That's a role I can do."

Her brothers had kids, after all ... although her experience with those kids was limited. Her role in her nieces' and nephews' lives involved little more than mailing birthday cards and Christmas presents. Since she lived hours away, they'd never so much as done an overnight at her place. When she visited her hometown, she stayed with her father, not her brothers and their families. Her dad and two of her brothers, families in tow, had visited while she'd been recovering earlier this year, but to avoid being a burden, they'd stayed in a hotel.

Still.

Piper had taken in her nephew when he'd needed her.

And now Neenah was taking in Kaylie. It didn't have to change everything about her personality or turn her into something she wasn't. In fact, it was better for everyone involved if it didn't.

Chapter Four

Twenty minutes after sunset, when Cody should've been leaving the station on Monday evening, a resident reported the theft of their outdoor Christmas decorations. A second call came in as he drove to the scene of the first. The third theft wasn't discovered until an officer knocked on doors, seeking reports of unusual activity from the neighbors. The fourth, when a man returned home from work, saw all the activity, and realized that his own house should be aglow.

Investigating a whole neighborhood of missing decorations would take a while. Good thing Cody had nowhere else to be. Neenah had returned home on Friday, and they'd texted regularly, but she'd asked for a few days to get Kaylie settled. She'd agreed to meet him at the gym tomorrow, and that promise would have to tide him over.

He trained the beam of his flashlight on the coal. "He escalated."

Justin McKinnon's radio interjected with updates about an unrelated incident across town. The officer turned it down. He'd only been on the force about a year, but the former ball player had proven to be hardworking and dedicated to justice. "Still suspect a prank?"

"Garrett told you about that?"

Justin gave a single nod.

Cody scanned the shadowed street. "It was one thing when just one nativity set disappeared. Stealing this many decorations could amount to a felony if they're all charged together."

Justin pointed with his flashlight toward the edge of the property. "There's only a trail of coal where the light strings were. They don't lead anywhere past the four properties that were hit."

Cody had noticed the same. The coal ran along bushes and houses and trees, as though the wires had been lowered to the ground and turned to fossil fuel. Little piles of it sat where inflatables had been. Similar to the scene where the nativity figurines had been stolen, the footprints suggested a monster of some kind. "It's the same with the prints?"

"Yep. They're on the properties by the stolen decorations. There are some prints crossing yards and into the street, but no obvious place where he changed or came or went."

Down the block, a car slowed and swung into a driveway. Justin consulted his notes. "Haven't talked to anyone at that address yet."

As he headed off to meet the homeowner, Cody shifted his flashlight. He could understand not noticing the absence of lights during the day. The missing inflatables were a little harder to excuse. Shouldn't the homeowners have noticed sometime before nightfall? But okay, nobody did. Sometimes, the absence of things was harder to pick up on than the presence of something that didn't belong.

Which brought him to the odd footprints. If nothing else, a kid walking to or from school should've spotted those and come home telling tall tales that inspired someone to look outside.

He made his way down the street and joined Justin, who stood nearby as the homeowner tapped his phone screen.

"Oh, wow." The man shifted his face closer to the device, and the glow glinted off his wide eyes. "You guys aren't going to believe this." He offered them the phone.

Cody accepted it.

A furry white figure hovered at the edge of the screen, the footage paused.

He flicked a look at the homeowner, in case this was a prank after all and the guy was in on it. But his brow knit and his eyes anxiously trained on them like he wanted answers as much as they did.

Cody hit the play icon, and the snow monster moved across the screen, carrying a cardboard box piled high. The fabric flopping over the edge of the container could be an inflatable. A plug and wire dangled, too, swinging with each step.

Justin leaned even closer. "So the Abominable Snowman did it."

"And no one noticed a full yeti costume?" Cody rubbed his forehead.

With a layer of snow and lights glowing in the windows, the neighborhood appeared peacefully tucked in for the night. A little dark for the Christmas season, though. The thief yeti had packed up every light string, velvet bow, moving reindeer, and inflatable Santa on the whole block.

To the residents' credit, it was possible no one had been out last night when the thefts occurred—two a.m., according to the timestamp. And if someone had passed by, a figure in a textured white getup could drop to the ground and resemble a snow-covered bush.

Cody returned the phone and offered his card to the homeowner. "Can you send the footage to me?"

"Sure thing. I'll email it right away."

He and Justin headed back toward their cars.

"People are going to have a field day with this when word gets out it's a yeti," Justin said.

That seemed to be what the perpetrator wanted. Why else be so theatrical about the whole thing? But who knew what the public's reaction would be.

People might urge each other to install cameras to aid in the apprehension of the perpetrator. Alternatively, they might patrol the streets themselves. That idea didn't sit well. The thief may not have proven dangerous—yet—but the situation could escalate if vigilantes took things too far.

Last, because humor did tend to win people over, the public might side with the yeti. If that happened, the police would lose respect, rendering any number of investigations more difficult. Not only would his father be angry, but more property owners would suffer loss, and the potential for a copycat with less playful antics would increase.

One yeti running around town was quite enough.

* * *

Had Neenah been making people feel unimportant for years?

Many times while on the force, work kept her late, so she ran behind on other commitments. She'd also ducked out of countless functions early to report for shifts. Cody must've understood because he was in the same boat. But other people? Because now that she no longer had that demand on her time, and Cody was the one texting he'd be late, she felt the bruise of rejection.

Which was, of course, ridiculous.

He had a job to do. He'd already done her the favor of

buying her this gym membership. So what if he was going to be late the first time they met here?

Yet, after several days apart—especially considering so much had happened—she needed a refill of his calm confidence in her decision to take in Kaylie. And if the newspaper headline could be believed, he had some stories of his own to tell.

Biding her time until he arrived, she carried her things—a newspaper, a water bottle, and a towel—to the elliptical machines. Though she preferred the treadmills, her knees demanded she choose the lower-impact activity. A few women used the machines, ponytails swishing.

She chose an elliptical and stepped up. She wouldn't need the newspaper until Cody arrived, so she folded it around her water bottle and stuffed both in the cup holder. She draped the towel over a stationary piece of the machine and eased into moving her feet.

"Oh, hey, Neenah."

At the bright voice, she looked to the elliptical next to hers.

Clara, the community relations officer, let go of the handle to wave.

"I didn't know you worked out here. Why don't you use the station's fitness center?"

"Everyone there's too serious about working out. Like, are we staying in shape or qualifying for the Olympics? I prefer to be among the normal people." Clara sucked in air, her pace proving she wasn't a slouch about fitness herself. "So, I've been dying to ask."

Neenah selected a workout and started the warm-up. "Ask what?"

"Now that you don't work together, are you and Cody finally going to be a thing?"

"We're friends." Brushing off inquiries about her relationship with Cody had been easier before she'd come to depend on him the way she had this year. And before she'd lost all good sense and almost kissed him. Now, her denial of more between them came out like a shifty witness lying on the stand. She moved her feet faster, as if that would allow her to outrun this conversation.

How she missed runs out in the real world.

"The man dotes on you. And if I'm not mistaken, you're pretty attached to him too."

"I've needed a lot this year. That's been hard for me, and I'm grateful for everything he—and everyone else—has helped me with. That's all you're noticing."

Or so she could hope, even if the emotion she'd felt during that hug last week hadn't been gratitude. But even that hiccup of attraction could be blamed on the long year, her retirement, and her concern over taking in Kaylie. Her brain and emotions were overloaded. Of course they swerved unpredictably. She didn't need to let her whole life go any further off the rails because of one renegade bout of attraction. "We're just friends."

"Right, but wasn't that because Chief Adams made you?"

Her feet slowed on the pedals. "Chief Adams made us be friends?"

"Made you limit yourselves to friendship. I, um, well, the walls in the station aren't exactly thick. I heard that speech he gave you."

Neenah had classified the only speech that came to mind as top secret. She'd never revealed it to anyone. Yet someone had overheard? Clara would've mentioned such a juicy conversation years ago, surely. Best to play innocent.

"What speech?" With the entirety of the English language at her disposal, all she seemed capable of was parroting back what Clara said and adding a question mark at the end. She pointed her focus back on her display and selected harder settings. Perhaps an intense workout would cover a multitude of tells.

Clara swished along at a slower pace that allowed the interrogation to continue. "Yeah, years ago. Honestly, I figured there was no way you'd let Chief have his way, but here we are, and you and Cody still haven't acted on all that chemistry."

"You overheard ..." She couldn't bring herself to say it. If Clara had heard something different from what she suspected, she didn't want to add any details.

"The whole speech about how he discourages his officers from dating, and if you and Cody want to reach your potential at the station, you'll avoid complicating your professional lives with personal drama."

Wow. Clara had heard—and retained—a lot. Back then, she and Neenah hadn't known each other as well. They still weren't close friends, but they'd bonded some over the years. This wasn't the first time Clara had brought up Cody, but it was the first time she'd revealed how much she knew.

"I was new at the time," Clara continued. "I thought about quitting if the chief was going to be so controlling, but then I found out Cody's his son and figured that was why he got so involved. But isn't it crazy that he'd talk about his own son's love life and career in a way that I didn't even know they were related? And why in the world wouldn't he want his son with you? You're like, the gold standard, and you're perfect for each other."

"Why would you say that?"

"This year hasn't proven it to you? He was *wrecked* when you got hurt. He'd do anything for you, and you for him."

The weight Clara put on the word "wrecked" added a few more levels of difficulty to the elliptical. The weeks following her accident were a blur of painkillers, appointments, and surgeries. She'd noted Cody's caring presence—and owed him for it—but she hadn't been in a place mentally or physically to notice the toll the accident and its aftermath might've taken on him.

Clara wasn't finished. "He instantly used vacation and trades and whatever it took to be the one to drive you to and from your appointments and surgeries. A lot of us offered to do more, but he only let other people help when he had to."

Those other people must've gone to Cody and not her, because she would've spread the load more. She'd felt like such a burden to him. And here, he'd chosen his involvement.

"Why did you never tell him about his dad?" Clara's low question was barely audible over the whir of the ellipticals.

"What's to tell?"

"That his dad threatened both your jobs to keep you apart."

That wasn't exactly what he'd said. He'd suggested a relationship would prevent them from receiving promotions.

"Or maybe ..." Clara sighed wistfully. "That's the sacrifice you made, not complicating his relationship with his father or standing in the way of his career."

Both reasons played into it, but she wasn't sure her sacrifice balanced even half of what Cody had done for her this year, in part because she'd also been concerned for her own career. And their friendship, which was so vital to her.

"It's tragic," Clara said. "He doesn't know the ways you've been shielding him this whole time. But now that you're not working there, his dad's complaint doesn't hold up, right? He was against officers dating, and you're not one anymore. So ..." Still gliding along, she shimmied her shoulders. "Possibilities abound. Oh!" Carla pointed toward the front door. "Speaking of ..."

Cody was two steps inside, and Neenah and Clara weren't the only women to notice him. Two others passed him on their way out and turned to ogle him once he'd stepped by. He'd been blessed with good genes, and he took his workouts seriously, as though he had as much to prove as Neenah did. Perhaps he did. She'd been at a disadvantage as a small woman in a sometimes-physical career. His disadvantage was a hard-to-please father. Oblivious to the attention he'd garnered, he continued while the women behind him traded guilty smiles and laughter.

"Shameless," Clara tsked. "Checking out your man like that."

"He's not mine." Neenah's chuckle sounded airy and unconvincing.

"Oh, honey." Clara stopped her machine. "He is, and everybody but you and those women know it."

Clara bustled away before Neenah could come up with a coherent argument otherwise.

Cody's gaze connected with hers, and the serious planes of his face transformed as his eyebrows lifted and a smile took over. Her brain replayed their hug—right down to musing about kissing him. The elliptical suddenly decreased the resistance, progressing through the program, and she nearly tipped backward. With a renewed grip on the handles, she focused on the display.

Back when she'd first given in to Chief Adams's objections, she'd expected her feelings for Cody to fade quickly. They hadn't exactly, but she'd kept them under control. Until recently. It had to be proximity—he'd been around a lot more this year—combined with no longer working for his father, as Clara had said.

But there were other factors to consider. Factors against giving in to these feelings. For example, she and Cody had only been close friends for six or seven years. Her parents had been married for ten before Mom split, proving even long-term affection didn't mean a couple could guarantee their feelings till death do us part. She was doing them both a favor by not allowing their friendship to shift gears.

He disappeared into the locker room. While he was gone, she half-heartedly continued her workout and pulled the newspaper from where she'd stuffed it next to her water bottle. She draped it over the display of her elliptical, the front-page headline bold.

Cody emerged a few minutes later in gym shorts, a T-shirt, and sneakers, and headed her way. "Sorry I'm late."

"It's fine." And it was. Either the feeling of rejection had faded like the overreaction it was, or simply being in his presence erased the sting. "They don't have any treadmills beside ellipticals, so we would've had to split up for cardio anyway."

"I would've used an elliptical."

She didn't doubt it. He would rearrange his whole life for her and be happy about it. But even she didn't want to make the adjustments her body now required, so why subject him to that? "I'm almost done here."

He circled her machine, probably to check the settings and gain some clues about her workout. Instead of information, all he would find was the headline she'd displayed for him: *Police Seek Criminal Yeti.*

She knew the moment he saw, because he grunted.

She grinned. "Bet you're regretting using the word 'yeti' when the newspaper called for a quote. Is the station overrun with sightings?"

He crossed his arms, and she looked away from the flex and play of muscles and tendons. "The public relations officer will field all media inquiries moving forward."

A little late now for such careful wording. "Chief's orders?"

He rubbed the back of his neck. "The perpetrator stole over two thousand dollars' worth of decorations in less than a week, so it can be charged as a felony. It should be taken seriously." His line of sight locked on the headline, and the corners of his mouth tightened.

This wasn't as fun as she'd hoped it would be. "Did Chief actually give you a hard time?"

He raised his eyebrows and looked away, a silent confirmation. If Chief had been disappointed, that didn't bode well for Cody's bid for the detective role.

She slowed her pace, collected the paper and her water bottle, and hopped down. "You'll catch the guy."

He pressed his mouth into a thin line. "What's this I hear about you interviewing to be a bouncer at The Mesa?"

So he was fighting fire with fire. Fair enough.

Neenah mopped her face with her towel as they made their way past the treadmills. "Shouldn't you be asking me about Kaylie?"

He dropped his head and nodded. "How's Kaylie?"

"Most of the time, she seems good. We got her room all set up, and I've shown her around town some, but it's almost too good. She's usually upbeat, but she didn't want to weigh in on what food I keep around the house or what we do. She says she's okay, but if she won't even tell me whether she prefers eggs, cereal, or oatmeal for breakfast, how can I believe that?"

"It's early days. Trust takes time. So does grieving."

Neenah knew those things in theory but struggled to internalize them when faced with a teen she longed to care for well. The reassurances helped. The fact that she couldn't trace whether that was because they were true or because Cody had been the one to say them did not. "One of her hobbies is calligraphy. Her mom was into that kind of thing too. Wanted to start a stationery company but never followed through. Anyway, Kaylie transcribes Bible verses. That's what she was doing when I left to come here."

"That should be helpful."

"I hope so." She was working on Psalm 23 and had several other comforting passages pinned to her bedroom walls already.

"You two are going to figure it out." He took a seat on a rowing machine.

She claimed the one next to him, and they fell into rhythm.

In her peripheral vision, Cody's face angled toward her. "Being a bouncer could be just as hard on your knees as being a cop."

Her shorts left the scars zippering up her knees on full display. She pressed with her legs and rowed backward, picking up the pace, but as her knees straightened, the scars appeared deeper. "Only if a situation gets out of control, and if I do my job right, it would never come to that."

"You know how I know you were out there."

"I assume Quince told you." As she'd been leaving the interview, the officer had crossed the parking lot to enter the building. She hadn't hung around to ask what business had brought Cody's competition for the detective position to the honky-tonk, mostly because she hadn't wanted word to get around about her being there. The prospect of being a bouncer wasn't exactly a point of pride.

"Someone fired a gun in the parking lot." Cody matched her pace to keep himself level with her. "They haven't gotten an ID on the guy yet."

"Anyone hurt?"

"Could've been. A lot of people were around."

"Not that many if I haven't heard about it."

"You've been otherwise engaged."

Yet she'd heard about the yeti. Bringing that up might give her an edge in the argument, but she'd already poked enough fun at him. She wasn't out to wound him. Not when he only brought up The Mesa out of concern for her.

"I could handle The Mesa. I've navigated plenty of high-stakes situations."

"One of which forced you into retirement."

So much for not wounding each other.

She stopped rowing, dropped her feet to the ground. Clara was wrong; this would never work. While they'd both been on the force, his dad stood between them. Now that she was off, he considered her fragile. Less than she'd once been.

If he had a feeling for her, it was pity, and that hurt worse than her knees ever did.

"I have to go." She walked away.

Chapter Five

So maybe she'd been rude to leave like that, but Neenah had done them both a favor. Spending time with Cody before she cooled down would've resulted in spewing things she didn't mean. Unfortunately, since she hadn't asked for a specific amount of time to herself, he would follow her shortly in search of a resolution.

On reaching home, she hooked up her horse trailer and invited Kaylie along to collect her mare from Price Quarter Horses. Neenah had arranged for a week of boarding to allow herself and Kaylie an adjustment period before adding BeeBee's care to their routine. They could handle the added responsibility now, and the task kept her from home—and Cody—for an extra hour.

Sure enough, though. When she turned onto her street, a hulking black truck dominated her driveway and blocked the two-track lane to the barn.

Cody left her front porch and backed his truck out of her way.

"Who's that?" Kaylie asked.

"My friend Cody." Hopefully, planting the label early would

set the tone for later so Kaylie wouldn't jump back on the *do-you-like-him* train after he left. Or, horror of horrors, *before* he left.

"Is he the one who's been texting you?"

"Yes." Neenah steered past his truck and down the rutted lane to the barn.

"Are you two fighting?" Kaylie asked.

"Why do you ask?"

"Because I usually text my friends back. Plus, you kind of glared at him as you passed."

For not liking police, this girl possessed keen observation skills and didn't mind calling people out.

"We're not fighting." Fighting implied a heated exchange of words. Or worse, physical blows.

"If you say so." Kaylie twisted to look backward out her window. "He got out. He's coming this way."

"I'm sure he wants to meet you." Neenah parked so the trailer opened near the barn's entrance.

As she hopped from the driver's seat, a rumble informed her that Cody rolled open the barn door. BeeBee whinnied, happy to be home.

Kaylie met Neenah by the back of the trailer. The girl's eyes tracked movement beyond Neenah, alerting her to Cody's advance before she heard the crunch of his footfall.

And then, his familiar deep voice. "You must be Kaylie."

The teen gave a little wave. "Yup. Hi. Cody?"

If he answered her, he did so silently. "How are you liking Redemption Ridge?"

"Everything's so nice. And it's about to get nicer. Neenah says BeeBee can keep up with me on runs, so we'll get to go together." The girl launched into explaining their plan for Neenah to ride and Kaylie to run.

Neenah stepped into the trailer and stroked her horse's neck. "Welcome home, BeeBee."

The mare nosed her shoulder, and Neenah leaned into her warmth for a restorative breath. If BeeBee noticed a difference since the accident, she didn't hold it against her.

"All right. Let's back up. Back."

Thanks to being trailered regularly for rides all over the Western Slope, BeeBee backed out of the trailer beautifully.

With the walls no longer blocking eye contact, Cody met her gaze with a wince of apology.

She sighed, and her anger washed out with her breath. Should he really have to grovel when he'd only spoken the truth? She *had* sustained life-changing injuries the last time she'd been in danger. She was a lot less capable of protecting and caring for herself than she'd always imagined. Maybe she had no business staying in the security sector.

She nodded her forgiveness before forcing a smile for Kaylie. "I'm going to groom BeeBee, then walk her around the paddock, if you want to help."

"Oh yes!" Kaylie bounced alongside her into the barn.

Once she had BeeBee in the crossties, she showed Kaylie how to use a rubber curry comb before taking the second one to BeeBee's other side.

Cody leaned a shoulder into the wall and toyed with a piece of hay. "Have you had much experience with horses, Kaylie?"

Neenah braced herself. With one so fresh from tragedy, any conversation might hit on difficult subjects.

"I've always wished I did." Kaylie's wistful voice blended with the quiet swish of the brushes. "My mom used to be a rodeo trick rider. She said her horse was her best friend in high school, but they're expensive and we lived in town, so ..." She ran a hand over BeeBee's coat.

Cody's blue eyes flickered, clearly monitoring Kaylie's body language and mood. "There are a lot of horses in this area. Not only BeeBee here, but did you get to see the herd at Price Quarter Horses?"

Tension released from Neenah's shoulders. He'd eased the conversation away from the painful topics of her mother and the life she'd been forced to leave behind and focused instead on some of the beauty nearby.

"Seems like they have a bunch of them, so I guess?" Kaylie seemed to note that Neenah had made more progress and redoubled her efforts to keep up.

"You probably saw the ones up by the stables," Cody said. "The family has a herd that lives off on the property. It's something to see. This time of year, they have to drop off hay for them. I bet Hollis would bring you and Neenah along one day if you wanted."

"Oh yeah?" Kaylie's hair swung like shifting sunbeams as she glanced at Cody. "That would be fun."

More of Neenah's frustration with him dropped away. He didn't even like horses. The only reason he knew anything about the routines at Price Quarter Horses was that he'd accompanied her there on a couple of trail rides. "I'll talk to Hollis," she promised.

They moved through the various brushes, and he continued with his careful navigation of conversation. It was hard to decide which touched her more, Kaylie's doting attention for BeeBee or Cody's concern for her new ward.

She'd seen that softness around his eyes a few times before. Once when he'd reunited a lost child with her parents. Another time as he returned a stray cat to its elderly owner— despite the red scratches covering his arms.

Winding down, Neenah traded her dandy brush for a face brush, then extended the soft-bristled tool toward Kaylie. "Would you like to do the honors? This is her favorite."

With her hallmark enthusiasm, Kaylie joined her at BeeBee's head.

As soon as Neenah touched the brush to her forehead, BeeBee lowered her face and closed her eyes, settling in to be pampered. Once she'd demonstrated the technique, she let Kaylie take over.

Meanwhile, Cody's eyes tracked back and forth between them. "You ladies going to the barn dance?"

"Wasn't planning on it," Neenah said.

But at the same time, Kaylie asked, "What's that?"

Neenah shot him a warning look, but his powers of observation conveniently failed.

He dropped the hay and dusted his hands against each other. "It's a dance put on every year by one of the big ranches. The whole town goes. It's pretty much the start of the Christmas season in Redemption Ridge. Most ladies use it as an excuse to buy a fancy dress."

Kaylie turned hopeful eyes on Neenah. "That sounds fun."

"It's on Saturday," Cody supplied. "There're a couple of stores in town that might have dresses."

If he was such an expert, he should take her. Neenah had gone dress shopping all of one time in Redemption Ridge and had worn the same dress to the annual barn dance ever since. Although that dress showed her knees. If she was going to attend this year, she'd want a different one.

Kaylie must've read her distaste for browsing racks of satin and tulle, because she clasped her hands below her chin and changed course. "I don't even need a new one. It's not like anyone around here has seen the ones I wore back home."

BeeBee nudged the girl's forearm, reminding her to get back to the pampering session.

"Sorry, honey." Kaylie ran the brush over the horse's cheek, then peeked at Neenah. "Please?"

She'd promised to share her social life with Kaylie. Though she didn't want to play dress-up and attend the dance, she also wouldn't be the one to squash Kaylie's excitement. "Okay. We'll go. We can even look at a few dresses."

After Kaylie had run the brush over every hair on BeeBee's face at least three times, she returned it to Neenah. "I haven't seen some of my makeup and hair stuff yet, and I'll need it for the dance, so I'm going to unpack some more."

She trotted off, and Cody's attention settled on Neenah. Forget butterflies in her stomach. It felt like her lungs themselves fluttered with nerves at the prospect of finishing the conversation she'd walked away from.

She put the grooming tools away and unhooked BeeBee from the crossties. "BeeBee's only been gone a week, but I'd like to walk the paddock to make sure no critters moved in and dug holes while she was gone."

Cody kept pace with her as they stepped into the fenced area behind the stable, BeeBee's head bobbing between them. "I'm sorry for bringing up your injury."

"That's not what bothered me. The problem was the implication I couldn't handle myself. What happened to me could've happened to anyone. My whole life shouldn't have to change because of it."

"I know you can handle yourself."

"So why are you trying to limit me?"

A low, rueful laugh rumbled in his throat. "It's not about limiting."

"Then what?"

"You've already sacrificed for the greater good." Passion growing, his words rushed along like a river drumming against boulders. "I don't want you to give up more. It was too much as it is."

"No, it wasn't." Her own depth of feeling spurted out in more of a geyser, voice rising. "You would've gone through the same thing to do your job and to do it well."

Cody's hand caught hers on the lead, and he kept

BeeBee from advancing between them as he squared his stance to Neenah. "Do you want to know what I'd go through if it'd spare you this whole experience? To do it over and cover the back of the house myself?" His body radiated tension.

BeeBee shifted back, but Neenah froze, torn between fear of what might happen to their friendship if they made a misstep and longing for him to verbalize the current of care she thought she saw sparking in his blue eyes.

Withdrawing from the connection of eye contact was as difficult as letting go of a live wire. Success left her shaken, lonely. She peered into the understanding brown of BeeBee's eyes and stroked the horse's nose.

The mare's sweet presence weakened the pull between her and Cody and finally allowed his words to sink in. At the thought of him suffering the way she had, her head started to shake, propelled more by reflex than reason. "You being hurt would be even worse than me."

Yellow grass swished as he took half a step toward her. "Why?"

"Because ..." She wouldn't wish the pain she'd experienced on her enemies, let alone on her best friend. She'd never felt safer on patrol than when he was with her. They checked on each other after rough incidents. To help him recover from a particularly traumatic call, she'd once spent every non-working waking hour with him for two weeks. He'd been invaluable during her recovery this year.

He—his wellbeing—mattered to her. They needed each other.

And though perhaps she was shallow to even think it, Cody took care of himself. If musculature and form like his weren't evidence of an artful Creator, nothing was. No one, let alone one of its biggest admirers, would throw a master-piece in front of a speeding car.

Not that she could tell her best friend she considered him a work of art.

"Policing is your life too," she said. "I know how much it means to you to prove yourself to your dad."

"Your dad is a cop too."

"It's not the same. He's always been proud of me." Her gaze flicked to him, checking whether he understood she laid the fault at his father's feet and not his own.

His unwavering focus suggested he hadn't thought of himself at all. "I've always been proud of you too. But that doesn't mean I've ever wanted to leave you to fend for your-self. If you get into trouble at The Mesa, I can't be there. I don't want to limit you. I just wish I could keep you safe."

If only she could tell him how hearing those words from him stilled a deep-seated uneasiness that lurked in her belly. Though she knew the futility of such wishes, at least she wasn't alone in them, and no one's company comforted her more than his. "I appreciate that." More than she could say.

She'd never felt so lost in her life, and turning to Cody as the hero who could save her had never been more attractive, but decisions made during times of turmoil could only lead to chaos.

The hero she was supposed to turn to was Jesus.

If Cody really did wish they could trade places, he needed to hear that too.

"Protecting each other is nice when it works out." She stroked BeeBee's forehead once more, then dropped her hand. "But it's God we really need to trust through it all. What I really need from you—and what I hope to give—is support. Not protection. I already have enough limitations without you adding to them."

Cody took a long breath, then resumed their walk. "Maybe it's time I take on a second job."

"At The Mesa?"

"I'd bring in some extra cash, hang out with my best friend …"

He was hopeless.

And she was flattered.

She might as well let him off the hook. "The Mesa called. They hired someone else."

Cody's gaze slid to her, eyes narrowed, but the corners of his mouth twitched like he couldn't decide whether to be annoyed or amused she hadn't told him sooner. Or maybe he was simply happy she wouldn't be keeping drunken cowboys in their place.

"I am still planning to find something in security of some kind, so don't act too smug."

"Wouldn't dream of it."

"Yes, you would."

He chuckled, and the sound coaxed a laugh from her dry throat. They returned to the stable and settled BeeBee in for the night before walking the two-track back toward the house.

She bumped his arm with her shoulder. "I miss this. Feeling normal."

Even if only for a few minutes.

"Me too. That's why the barn dance is a good idea." He gave her a smile, but sadness poisoned it. "You haven't been spending as much time with friends this year, and I know people have missed seeing you. Plus, I'm sure it's not good for Kaylie to isolate."

"In that case, the barn dance isn't a long-term solution."

"A counselor wouldn't be the worst idea."

"For her or me?"

Cody shrugged.

Both, then.

Was he getting tired of being her anchor in all of this?

Maybe, despite not pursuing more, their relationship had changed. She wasn't used to not knowing where they stood with each other. It had been simple when they worked the same job, when there weren't so many tender feelings in play on both sides. When she could take care of herself, and they could pick on each other without worrying about breaking something.

Having a counselor to work through the worst of her struggles with could put less strain on their friendship, allowing them to glimpse a little of the normal she missed. "I'll look into it."

"And in the meantime, the barn dance."

She didn't want to go. She didn't enjoy dancing, and she had no good updates for all the well-meaning people who'd ask what she was up to now that she wasn't on the force. But she did usually attend. So for another glimpse of normal, as fleeting as it was sure to be, she promised to attend.

* * *

As song after song played and people milled around in the festively decorated barn, Cody almost texted Neenah to ask where she was. The dance had started half an hour ago, and she and Kaylie had yet to put in an appearance. But maintaining their friendship required a careful balance. After acting like she couldn't handle herself in a bouncer job, he needed to be on his best behavior. That meant not nagging her.

Instead of texting, he chatted with Piper and Graham and watched their son, Jasper, get more cupcake frosting on his face than in his mouth. Meanwhile, Graham offered baby Opal a bottle, and she set about draining it.

Finally, Neenah's confident stride navigated between the tables toward them. She usually wore a simple, knee-length black dress to this event. Because it was the only dress he'd ever seen her in, he'd assumed she only owned the one. But today, she wore a long gray dress. Also unusual for her, she wore smoky eye makeup and her hair down with her dark locks curled.

Kaylie shadowed her, clearly the one to thank for coaxing Neenah out of her shell. The girl's hair was styled the same way, and she, too, wore a healthy dose of eyeshadow. But instead of confidence, Kaylie had her arms pinned to her sides like she wanted to disappear. Pink tinged the whites of her eyes, noticeable even in the dim room. But probably only if someone was really looking.

Cody stood, and Neenah's brown eyes flicked to him, a little wide. Unsure.

"Who do we have here?" Piper asked.

Their friends all knew the circumstances and Kaylie's name, but Neenah made official introductions. Cody waved over Bryce, Piper's nephew, who had shot up the last year or two, so he was almost eye-level with Cody. The moment the teen spotted Kaylie, his eyes locked on her so firmly, he ran into a chair.

Kaylie jumped at the racket, and Neenah broke off what she'd been saying. The second her eyes landed on Bryce, a relieved smile took over her countenance. "Oh, good. Bryce, I'd like you to meet Kaylie. She's new here. She'll be attending your school as soon as the paperwork goes through."

Bryce's hands disappeared in his pockets. "Hey."

"Hi." Kaylie fiddled with her little purse.

That was it? The extent of their social skills?

Before Cody could intervene, Piper did. "Kaylie, Neenah said you run cross-country?"

She nodded.

"Bryce, one of your friends does too, right?"

"Yeah. Tori. She's over there." Bryce thumbed back the direction he'd come. "You want to go meet her?"

"Um, sure." Kaylie's wobbly smile said she was anything but *sure*, yet the pair headed off.

Cody watched until, when they were a few yards away, the kids started talking. Not having an audience of adults might've been all the help they needed.

Neenah sank into a chair. Cody scooped up his cup of cider, left the spot beside Graham, and circled the table. He'd been claiming seats near Neenah for so long, no one batted an eye as he settled next to her. Not touching her, of course, but close enough to catch the fruity scent of her shampoo.

"How are you and Kaylie adjusting to life together?" Piper asked.

"As well as can be expected." Neenah's lips formed a tense squiggle. "Getting ready to come here reminded her of homecoming, which reminded her of her mom, who did her makeup that day. I offered to stay home, but after she had some time, she wanted to be around people."

"Poor girl." Piper caressed her four-year-old son's head. "It's hard enough, losing a parent. I can't imagine how she feels without other family to fall back on."

Neenah peered after the teen. "I'm praying she makes lots of friends. She seems like a hardcore extrovert. That should help."

Several tables away, Kaylie's shoulders hadn't relaxed much, but one of Bryce's friends chatted with her, hands moving and face animated. If nothing else, she was getting a warm greeting.

"And you?" Piper asked.

Neenah shrugged. "I have no idea what I'm doing, but we're muddling through."

Piper's gaze flicked to Cody. He'd asked the small business owner if there was a position for Neenah at Second Chances, but if Piper let on to Cody's involvement in the offer, he'd be back in the doghouse. He tried to convey a silent warning.

Piper tucked her hair behind her ears. "I hear you're job hunting."

Neenah let her shoulder blades fall against the chairback. "I interviewed for one job. Didn't get it. Not sure where to try next. I want something active, but I need the right balance."

"How about Second Chances? Working on the sales floor means a lot of walking around and moving inventory." The offer sounded natural enough, though she paired it with a furtive glance at Cody.

Neenah was too busy picking at the tablecloth to notice. "No offense, but unless you're looking to implement a new loss prevention protocol, a consignment shop isn't in my wheelhouse."

"Graham redid the layout of the store and our fitting room policies a few years ago. Ever since, we don't have a lot of theft. But I'm happy to train you for the sales floor. Or if that isn't your thing, you could refinish furniture to sell in the store."

"I imagine that involves kneeling."

Piper's eyes went wide, and her cheeks flushed. "Oh. Can you ...? Oh."

"I *can* kneel. It's just uncomfortable. And I should've been more specific. I want something active that's at least somewhat related to my criminal justice experience."

"You could be a PI." Piper waggled her eyebrows. "Oh! Or a bounty hunter."

Cody pressed his mouth shut. He'd been ready for her to give up on recruiting Neenah to the store, but did she have to go that far?

Neenah laughed. "Not a lot of demand for either of those in a town this size. Then again, I've been thinking I might have to go farther. A few places in Grand Junction are hiring security."

Grand Junction? Cody's lungs locked up. One rejection in, and she was already looking for a job in another city? What if she moved there? Instead of being able to swing by whenever he had a few extra minutes, trips to see her would take planning and hours in the car.

A wail pulled him from his thoughts. Opal had finished her bottle. Spit up clung to the towel draped over Graham's shoulder, and the baby's face scrunched and reddened as she waved her tiny fists.

Piper grabbed a napkin to help mop up and shot Cody and Neenah a laughing smile. "Save yourselves."

Neenah scooted her chair back but hesitated to rise. "Do you need us to get you anything?"

"With this diaper bag, we could survive World War III." Graham adjusted his arms around Opal, then blinked hard and tilted his head away. "And by the smell of it ..."

"Ew." Jasper paused picking crumbs off his cupcake wrapper to make a face.

Neenah popped to her feet. "That's our cue."

Leaving friends in crisis went against his training. Cody scanned their faces. Neither Piper nor Graham looked happy about the prospect of changing the diaper, but their expressions somehow also held tenderness. Graham touched his wife's shoulder as he headed toward the restroom with Opal still screaming in his ear. Piper shot Cody a wink as she took a damp napkin to Jasper's cupcake face paint.

They weren't in crisis at all. They were living a messy moment in happily ever after.

Cody could only hope to one day be so blessed.

He joined Neenah, who marched toward the dance floor. Did she intend to dance? They'd been paired up at both Graham and Piper's wedding and Hollis and Lucy's. Their duties in the wedding parties had landed them in each other's arms on the dance floor, but otherwise, they'd never ventured there together.

What would it be like to dance with her when choice, not obligation, brought them together? And if she did make that choice now, after all this time, did that mean she was open to a shift in their relationship? He didn't want to sabotage the moment by being too distant. Then again, he could only imagine how uncomfortable he'd make her by holding her a little too close.

She cleared the last table and skirted the dance floor.

Shouldn't have gotten his hopes up. "Where are we headed?" he asked.

"I see Milo over there." She pointed to a redheaded man at a bar-height table. "Redemption Lodge is one of the few places in town with security. Might as well check in before I cast a broader net."

This was good. She was trying to stay in town, and the clientele at Redemption Lodge tended to involve fewer belligerent drunks than The Mesa. Now if only she'd stop talking about broader nets.

Milo and his wife, Phoebe, greeted them with smiles.

Phoebe rubbed Neenah's shoulder. "How are you holding up?"

Cody expected Neenah to sidestep the subject, but she bit her bottom lip and focused on the therapist. "I'm doing okay, but actually, I recently lost an old friend."

Phoebe tsked sympathetically. "I'm sorry to hear that."

"I haven't been close with her in a long time, but I've been feeling it more than I expected to. She was so vibrant, and she left behind a daughter who had nowhere to go. Kaylie, her daughter, is living with me now, and I'd like to get her in some kind of grief counseling to help her process everything. Do you do anything like that?"

"Oh." Phoebe rubbed her forearms as if to ward off goose bumps. "This has to be a God thing. I'm running a bit of an experiment this year. Since the holidays can be rough for people who have lost loved ones, I put together a family-friendly horse therapy grief group on Mondays through the first week of January. You've only missed one. Would you and Kaylie like to join us?"

"*She* might."

Phoebe rubbed her shoulder again. "You're grieving too—the loss of your friend and other things. Besides, each child needs an adult to walk through the process alongside him or her. Aside from any benefit you might experience yourself, the course could be a way to establish good, open communication between you and Kaylie right off the bat."

Neenah's chest rose with a deep breath. She let it out slowly as she nodded. "Okay. How do we sign up?"

"Call me first thing on Monday, and we'll get you all squared away to join us that afternoon. It's going to be wonderful."

Neenah chewed her lip, less enthusiastic, but Cody knew her stubborn side. Now that she'd committed, there'd be no stopping her from attending with Kaylie. Her gaze flicked to Milo, but she hesitated. Was she feeling self-conscious after the discussion about counseling?

Cody needed her to find gainful employment in Redemption Ridge—the more her life moved to Grand Junction, the more likely she'd be to follow it. He broke the ice for her. "Milo, you guys have any openings on the security team at Redemption Lodge? I know a former police officer who's more than qualified."

"Actually, yes. We had someone from the overnight crew give his notice." Milo's hazel eyes shifted to Neenah. "The hours aren't ideal, but it's a reliable, steady job working with and for great people."

Finally, some light returned to Neenah's countenance.

Next to her, though, Phoebe cringed. "She has a ward to consider, Milo."

"Oh." His smile faltered, as did Neenah's.

"Unless she's old enough to be alone overnight?" Phoebe asked.

"I don't like that idea." Neenah ran her palms down her hips. "I guess I need something during the day."

"I'm sorry." Milo scratched his beard. "We don't have anything with daytime hours."

Neenah nodded once, and her throat worked with a swallow. "Understandable. If that changes, let me know."

Milo reached partway across the table. "Hey, I hear the tech school wants instructors. Do you have your master's degree?"

Neenah froze, so Cody dipped his head in confirmation. He hadn't put the guy up to this, but the suggestion couldn't be better timed.

"With that and real-world experience, you're exactly what they're looking for."

Her smile shook as she offered it, and she ducked away from the table. Was she embarrassed? Trying to hide tears?

Milo frowned after her. "Tell her I'm sorry? I didn't mean to ..."

"You couldn't have known. I mentioned the tech school position once too." He excused himself and followed her onto the dance floor. He wasn't sure where she'd meant to go, but she ran into a pair of dancers and jolted back around.

Her eyes were glossy. Or at least, that was what he thought he glimpsed in the second before she put up a hand and lowered her face, hiding, even from him. But they were in the middle of the crowd, and there was no subtle way out of this. If she didn't want to make a scene, they'd do best to hide in plain sight.

He risked touching her upper arm. "Let's dance."

"Cody." She shook her head and tried to step around him, but she nearly ran into another couple.

He took the hand she held by her face and drew her in. "Take a minute. I'll be your shield."

"People will talk." Still trying to hide her face, her body bumped against his.

At the contact, a surge of protectiveness told him to lock his arms around her, but that would be the fastest way to send her back out into the fray. He maintained the same casual hold he'd used the other times they'd danced together. "So let them talk. Friends are allowed to dance."

She grunted a protest, but she placed a hand on his chest instead of running away. Under his palm on her back, her ribs expanded and released. Her forehead tipped against his shoulder. To anyone who glanced over, she'd look snuggled up to him, content to cut herself off from the rest of the world.

She smelled like berries, and her hair brushed his hand on her back. If only he could run his fingers through the glossy strands and kiss her forehead. The most he could allow himself, however, was to hold her tighter for a moment he didn't dare stretch.

Chapter Six

Neenah kept the high mounting block beside her stable because it had been helping her into the saddle for months. One of these days, she'd have to stop resenting the thing for reminding her of what she'd lost—the ability to mount without a block at all. She fit her boot into the stirrup and swung a leg over onto BeeBee's back. As she settled in the saddle, a sigh released from her core. Her own limitations mattered less here because BeeBee remained as healthy as ever. She stroked her mare's neck in appreciation.

Kaylie, on foot a couple of yards away, pressed both palms against the sides of her helmet. "You're sure I need this?"

The black helmet did contrast with her pastel running gear, but Neenah nodded. "BeeBee is a good horse, but she weighs about a thousand pounds. We don't need an accident."

Bracing against a fence post for balance, Kaylie swung her leg from one side to the other like a pendulum in a dynamic stretch. "So we'll start at a walk through the field, and I can run when we reach the trail?"

"Yes, but BeeBee and I will revert to a walk anytime there's another person on the trail. If your speed is too different from

BeeBee's, that's okay. I'll keep you in sight, and you do your thing." From her higher vantage point, Neenah eyed the first stretch.

The route ran along the back of a residential neighborhood. Other trail users could appear at any time. Distant mountains edged the view like white lace. Closer, yellow and brown warmed the landscape, glistening with snow that had melted in the mid-morning sun.

They set off and soon hit their stride on the trail, Kaylie jogging and BeeBee alternating between a trot and a walk. The movement felt like freedom and hope. From what she'd heard, Kaylie hadn't done much running in the last few weeks, so perhaps this would be equally uplifting for her.

"I like horse therapy a lot better than the other kind." Despite the effort of running, Kaylie lifted her voice over the clop of hooves.

"Me too," Neenah admitted.

They'd completed their first group session the night prior. Simply meeting the horse they'd been paired with and beginning to form a bond had led them both to surprising observations by the end of the evening.

Phoebe concluded the session by asking everyone to share something they'd learned.

"Starting over is harder than I expected." Neenah had meant working with an unfamiliar horse, but even as she spoke, she saw the parallel in her life outside the stable too.

Which made Phoebe's response even more welcome. "It feels hard because it *is* hard. But the reward is sweet, and we don't work alone."

As Neenah repeated that to herself, internalizing the message and thanking God for never leaving her to fend for herself, Phoebe turned to Kaylie beside her. "What did you learn today?"

"I didn't grow up around horses, so the whole thing's

intimidating, I guess? I'm just super glad we don't have to do everything at once. Like, glad we didn't have to ride right away or anything."

Phoebe nodded encouragingly. "We don't have to do everything at once. We get to be in process and learn and grow into new things. That's wonderful, Kaylie."

The girl beamed under the praise, and her demeanor as they'd gone about the rest of their evening seemed calmer. More peaceful.

Could Neenah use a similar approach to help Kaylie outside of therapy too? Asking the girl what she'd learned as they went about their lives wouldn't be hard. But was it presumptuous and harmful when done by someone with no training?

Kaylie cast a long look up at Neenah. "My counselor at Bible camp introduced one of the boys' counselors as her friend, and I totally believed it."

A weird piece of history. Perhaps Neenah hadn't been the only one struggling for something to say.

"I found out later they were engaged." The effort to maintain their pace added an airy quality to Kaylie's voice. "Like, she lied because she didn't think I could handle it? That's just weird. Why would I care?"

Neenah licked her lips, at a loss. "You *seem* to care."

Kaylie's eyes cut to her again, and her ponytail swished the opposite direction. "You know what I mean. It's condescending."

"Okay. I get how that would be frustrating."

"It's fine. I'm over it." Her tone belied her words, but who was Neenah to argue? "Just ... Is the same thing happening again?"

"What?"

"You said you and Cody are friends, but you don't act like friends."

"Of course we do." She shifted in the saddle. Their time on the dance floor the other night hadn't seemed exactly like friends. She'd felt a little too safe. A little too cared for. A few too many butterflies. But nothing had happened between them that pushed them out of the friend zone. If something had, she wouldn't have felt so safe.

"You act like true love waiting to happen."

Neenah barked a laugh, and BeeBee's ears twitched. She patted her neck. "We're friends and that's all we've ever been. Remember, you've hardly seen us together."

"I saw you dance. And talk. And laugh. The whole night, he was never more than three feet from you, and he looks at you like you're the only girl in the world."

"First of all, no." Her best friend had better not be getting all googly-eyed over her. "Second, that's such a cliché."

"If a cliché looked at me like that, I wouldn't be complaining."

"You're fifteen."

"Almost sixteen. And then I'm allowed to date, remember."

Ahead, pedestrians advanced toward them. She slowed BeeBee to a walk. "If you want to turn into a cliché for your birthday, that's your business. I have other plans."

Kaylie, who had pulled ahead, grinned back over her shoulder. "Becoming a spinster is a cliché too." She sprinted, and puffs of dust appeared in her wake.

"Not all single women are spinsters," Neenah called after her. Didn't the next generation know that? What was the archaic term doing in her vocabulary at all?

Kaylie gave no sign of hearing, but the walkers eyed her as if she'd lost it.

She smiled hello anyway, but after a moment, embarrassment averted her gaze to the right. A junk collection behind someone's shed was becoming one with the land. The rotted-out car had a sapling growing out of the windshield. Garbage cans overflowed with cardboard and fabric, and weeds hemmed in a collection of wood and metal scraps. Most of it had faded to shades of brown or gray, otherwise, she never would've noticed the snatches of blue, yellow, and red.

She lifted herself from the saddle to get a better view. The color adorned an old light-up nativity set.

Neenah pulled her phone from a zippered pocket and snapped a picture.

"What's going on?" Kaylie called back. She'd stopped thirty yards ahead.

An explanation would have to wait until they didn't need to shout. Neenah captured a few more shots and texted them, along with her location, to Cody. Finally, she reached Kaylie. "There's a nativity set in all that junk that matches the description of stolen property."

"You're reporting them?"

"The sighting, yes. This case has been a mess for Cody. He needs a win. Plus, I'd be angry if someone stole something from my yard, and this is pretty close to home."

"Yeah, I suppose." Hands on her hips, Kaylie twisted to look back the way they'd come. "Do you know these people?"

"No. And it might be a coincidence. Those sets aren't exactly rare."

Neenah's phone chimed with a new message.

CODY

Interesting. Thanks.

See? Friends. If he was looking for more from her, he would've tried to start up a conversation. He hadn't, so she was safe. The thing that did need more monitoring? Her own neighborhood.

Whether or not these were the stolen decorations, plenty

of people had passed by. Someone should've mentioned these to law enforcement sooner.

What other obvious red flags were her neighbors overlooking that allowed crime in Redemption Ridge?

Perhaps now, while between jobs, she was in a unique position to improve the safety of the town in a way she'd never thought to do while she'd been on the police force.

* * *

Cody took the steaming boxes from his passenger seat and crossed the yard to knock on Neenah's front door.

Kaylie swung it open. "Pizza?" She stepped aside and motioned him in with a flourish. "Anyone with pizza is always welcome."

"That's not true," Neenah called from somewhere out of sight.

"Okay, not anyone." Kaylie lifted her chin along with her voice, projecting. "But a *friend,* for sure."

Suspicious. He stepped inside, and fresh pine overpowered the scents of garlic, tomatoes, and dough. A tree stood in the living room, not yet decorated. Neenah didn't usually go all out with a fresh tree—and neither did he—but for some reason he liked that Kaylie had brought out her festive side.

He delivered the pizzas and breadsticks to the dining table and flipped open the lids. "Gotta reward my sources for the tip they gave me today."

"We were right?" Neenah appeared with a large box labeled *Christmas* in her arms.

He'd help her with it, if only she allowed such things. "We recovered the nativity set, lights, and some other decorations. None of the inflatables, though. And there's a set of animated reindeer still unaccounted for."

Neenah set her load beside the tree, while Kaylie delivered

plates and sodas to the table. They sat down, and Cody blessed the food.

Afterward, he'd barely gotten his fingers under a slice of the three-meat pizza when Neenah asked, "And the yeti? Any clues about who it is?"

"We found more footprints, so he's committed to the costume, but whoever it is approached and exited on the trail where there are too many other sets of prints to follow. The homeowners are an elderly couple who barely make it to the mailbox at the end of the driveway, let alone out behind the garage."

Neenah passed the breadsticks. "Do they have any kids or grandchildren who might be up to no good?"

He'd wondered the same thing. "No family in the area, but anyone could've chosen a random home with signs of disrepair and stashed the stolen goods there. Some of the junk behind the garage has been there for decades. I'm glad someone with an eye for detail passed by."

Kaylie's cheek puffed out with a lump of food as she spoke. "She's going to be so much help."

"Help?" He looked to Neenah.

She'd skipped makeup, at least as far as he could tell. Her hair hung in a braid over her shoulder. Her flannel, T-shirt and jeans looked comfortable, but her facial expression did not.

"Help with what?" he asked.

Kaylie gulped. "She's starting a neighborhood watch. Isn't that the coolest?"

Resistance built within him. She'd been medically retired for a reason. And since when did she make plans without at least mentioning them to him?

"When did this happen?"

"You appreciated my tip about the decorations." Neenah lifted her eyebrows, her voice half teasing and half guilty.

"I did." Hearing from her had been the highlight of his day, even before he saw she'd sent a tip about his case.

"So what's with the face?" She used her pizza to motion at his head.

He relaxed the tension from his forehead, but his mouth refused to lift into a smile. He missed being her sounding board. Missed working together on the force. The neighborhood watch wouldn't be the same. She'd be out there with only a ragtag group of volunteers and 911 as backup. "Can you resist following up personally?"

"I did today, didn't I?"

Today's discovery hadn't been particularly urgent or dangerous.

"Observe and report," he said.

She took a swig of her soda. "I know the drill."

"Then I think it's a good idea." What choice did he have? She'd made up her mind, and when concern for her safety was his only objection, she'd never change it. "How far have you gotten with setup?"

"I registered with the police department, and I posted on one of those neighborhood-centered social media sites today. I'd like to have the first meeting sooner rather than later. Given everything that's going on, even if I can't talk people into doing patrols, making them more aware of suspicious activity could at least provide some leads."

Cody swallowed hard. "Patrols?"

"Just to observe and report."

"Not on foot, right?"

"During the day, sure. People go for walks all the time." She quirked an eyebrow with a mischievous smile that reminded him of the old days.

Back then, he'd enjoyed that look. Not so much since he'd gained memories of her on the ground with severe injuries.

"Unless you want me riding BeeBee through town? I was on horseback when I saw the stash of decorations."

"Just stay safe. Keep a distance if you see something suspicious. And if you decide to keep an eye out overnight, stay in your truck with the doors locked. Do not ever—"

She held up a hand to cut him off. "I lost my badge, not my mind."

"So, um ..." Kaylie's eyes had grown as big as the pizzas. "Is the neighborhood watch dangerous?"

Neenah cocked her head and glared at him as if to say, "Look what you've done now."

He *had* forgotten the teen's presence. He spared her a smile. "Redemption Ridge is generally a safe place to live."

Kaylie peered down at her half-finished pizza slice and slipped her hands under her thighs as splotches formed on her cheeks. "That's what they said about Mom's surgery too. More or less."

Neenah placed a hand on the table by Kaylie. "No one has been hurt in either type of theft—the home break-ins or the stolen decorations—and the better we all do in keeping an eye out for each other, the safer everyone and their belongings will be."

"Nothing can happen to you. I have, um ..." The red spread to cover her face and neck. "Nowhere else to go."

Neenah hauled her chair closer and wrapped an arm around her shoulders. "Nothing is going to happen to me."

Kaylie nodded meekly.

Neenah shot him daggers.

He deserved that.

After a couple of quiet minutes, Kaylie collected herself, Neenah returned her chair to its place, and the conversation rebounded. As they finished their meal, Kaylie invited him to stay to help decorate the tree.

"He's not exactly an expert." Neenah placed the leftover

pizza in the refrigerator. "He only puts out one decoration for Christmas."

"By choice." He had a shelf in his living room where he set a cross for Easter, a turkey figurine for Thanksgiving, and an antique ceramic Christmas tree that once belonged to his grandparents. "I'm capable of hanging lights and a few ornaments."

"Oh, it's so many more than a few. Wait until you see our collection." Kaylie disappeared down the hall toward her bedroom.

Cody fit their plates into the dishwasher. "Not sure you're in the place to judge my decorating skills. It's been years since I've seen a tree here."

"Just stating facts." Neenah leaned to see down the hall. Apparently deciding the coast was clear, she settled a hip against the counter and crossed her arms. "I got the tree for her. It was a tradition for her and her mom. She also wants to bake cookies tonight."

"Do you know how to bake cookies?"

"In theory. Her grandma sent us the recipe." A line appeared beside her mouth. "But none of this comes naturally to me."

"For knowing her so briefly, you seem to understand her pretty well."

She held his eye contact, hungry for reassurance. At least, that was how he read her expression, until her eyes widened and her neck tensed. She pushed away from the counter and averted her eyes.

What just happened?

"I know what it's like to lose a mother." She picked at the counter. "Different circumstances, since mine still sends a card or a text once in a while, but we lost the close mother-daughter dynamic when she left Dad, and no one filled the gap. My dad and brothers didn't even do hugs." She fit her fingers in her pockets, eyebrows at a pained slant that made him want to wrap her in his arms then and there.

But something about the shift he'd witnessed moments before left him uneasy.

Jingling sounded from the hall. That was the sound of a box of Christmas decorations if he'd ever heard one, and if he registered Kaylie coming, she was back in earshot.

He lifted his voice to ensure she heard. "I've been promised cookies if I stay, so I'm in."

A weak smile lifted Neenah's lips. Whatever had happened, she seemed grateful for his company. He'd hang on to that.

Chapter Seven

Two days later, reports of missing inflatables cropped up all over Redemption Ridge. Cody went from one scene to the next until a call came in that the home burglar struck too, this time targeting a large house in the newest neighborhood in town. Despite having only minutes before police responded to the home security system, he'd gotten away.

Justin met Cody and briefed him as they walked up the driveway. "Two big differences between this crime and the others. First, they had some new electronics—a TV and a gaming system—but they were saving them for Christmas, so they didn't have any visible evidence of the purchases sitting out like the others did." He pointed toward the garbage and recycling bins tucked against the garage, tidy and closed. "And we got him on camera."

"Yeah?" Fresh energy quickened Cody's step. "Is the footage any good?"

Justin winced. "I'll show you."

They walked through the scene, spoke with the home-owner, and watched the video. Set to record activity on the front step and not in the more distant driveway, the grainy images wouldn't be much help.

Back at the station, Cody pulled up the video on his monitor to see if increasing the size would supply any leads. White pickups like the one recorded ranked as one of the most common vehicles on the road. No one, including the camera, got a license plate. The figure who came and went from the house wore a thick winter jacket and a ski mask. Nothing distinctive stood out about his work boots, jeans, or black gloves.

By comparing the figure to the height of the truck, Cody estimated the burglar was five feet nine or ten inches. The average height of an American male. Weight? On the average side, either a little heavyset or wearing a too-big jacket.

If only cops could "clean up" awful footage the way TV shows portrayed. Stuck with real-world, small-town technology, he could conclude little but that Redemption Ridge was being plundered by polar opposites.

The burglar was average in every way. The yeti had monster feet and was covered in white fur.

Cody rubbed his face and went for more coffee in the breakroom.

"Heard your girlfriend got pulled over," Burt Quince crowed.

Cody did not envy whoever the guy had found to annoy today, but he wasn't about to cut in and deal with him himself. Competing for the detective role irked him enough. He added a sugar packet to what was sure to be a bitter brew.

"You hear me?" Quince asked.

No one responded.

Oh. It was just the two of them, so the girlfriend comment had been aimed at Cody. He swirled one of the wooden stir sticks through his cup. "Your intel's bad. I don't have a girlfriend."

"Neenah."

He hadn't wanted to give Quince an inch, but his eyebrows lifted almost that far. "Neenah got pulled over?" She usually kept close enough to the limit that no one would bother.

"Some teen girl was driving. Cue the waterworks, but she blew a stop sign."

Cody tossed the stir stick. "Who was the officer?"

"Johnson. Let her off with a verbal warning, which is less than I would've done."

"The girl is a new driver, still on her learner's permit."

"That's no excuse."

Rather than hang around and argue, Cody nodded once and stepped out of the breakroom. He didn't see Garrett Johnson around to ask for particulars about Kaylie and Neenah. Instead, he registered a white shape looming by his desk. Patrol officers wore dark-blue uniforms, making it the most common color in the room. Chief Adams's white uniform shirt made him stand out like a lone polar bear. The gold pins on the man's collar advertising his rank glinted as he inspected the fidget magnets Neenah gave Cody one Christmas.

Steeling himself for an even more difficult conversation than the one with Quince, Cody crossed the room.

His father returned the black and silver magnets to their stand and looked beyond him. "Officer Quince, join us."

Great. Double the fun.

Cody set his coffee on his desk and crossed his arms. His chair waited nearby, but rather than lower himself any further in Chief's or Quince's opinion, he remained standing.

"Sir?" Quince rested his hands on his duty belt.

"Good work on finding the shooter from The Mesa."

Quince stood straighter. "Thank you, sir."

Cody hadn't heard the case was closed. It couldn't be good

for him that Quince had closed at least two cases to Cody's zero.

Chief's blue eyes fixed on him. "What is the latest on your investigations?"

He recapped, starting with recovering the stash of decorations and ending with the description of the home burglar's truck and build.

"Have you been able to find a similarity between the houses that were hit?"

"Only that they all bought new electronics recently from the same store, Tech City. I'm looking into employees."

"It's possible each burglary was committed by a different party," Quince said.

"I'm keeping that in mind."

Chief clasped his hands. "Is it safe to say the Christmas decoration investigation has taken a backseat to the burglaries?"

"To an extent. The losses in the home burglaries are higher, and the charges more serious." His father would know that, but he needed Chief to know he had his priorities right.

Chief's focus shifted. "Quince, I'm assigning you to take over the stolen Christmas decorations."

"But—"

Chief cut Cody off with a lifted hand. "Fill him in." To Quince, he said, "I expect another closed case."

Quince bobbed his head. "I won't let you down, sir."

"See that you don't." He started away. "This yeti circus is bad for business."

On that, Cody agreed. An eccentric character getting away with a crime on his watch rankled him, but not as much as a burglar violating people's homes. Chief had left him with the more serious crime, but why assign the yeti to Quince?

The change might've been motivated by the simple fact that Quince had run out of investigative work. Or Chief might want Cody free to focus on the burglaries. But the third possibility didn't sit as well. Chief might think Quince could succeed where Cody had failed.

Whatever the case, Cody needed to find the burglar. His career, not to mention the safety of Redemption Ridge residents, depended on it—as did his ability to earn any respect from his father.

* * *

Neenah passed the clipboard to the nearest attendee of her inaugural neighborhood watch meeting. She'd opted to host this meeting at the rec center because she'd wanted room for plenty of residents to attend and get involved. When so many of the seats had filled up, she'd been encouraged. Then she'd realized most of the attendees were aged eighty or older. Their Seniors' Balance workout class had ended minutes before the neighborhood watch meeting began.

She'd take what she could get. Retirees were keen observers of their neighborhoods. Why not train them to watch for the right activity?

"I br—" Movement at the back of the room pulled her focus, and Cody stepped through the door. The sea of white hair and wrinkled faces contrasted with the vitality broadcast in his easy stride. He dipped his chin in a nod of greeting and dropped into a chair. Her stomach swooped like it was along for the ride.

Only too aware she stood in front of a room full of witnesses, she jerked her attention back to the task at hand. "I broke the schedule into hour-long slots to give flexibility, but if you're able to patrol a couple of hours in a row, that would help us cover more. While that's going around, I'll give you a few minutes to look over the handout, and you can let me know if you have any questions."

Papers shuffled.

Cody surveyed the room, his eyes narrowed with concentration as he cataloged details of her audience. Afterward, he would be able to identify any of her twenty-five attendees in a lineup.

The night he'd brought pizza and they'd found a moment alone to discuss how things were going with Kaylie, she'd soaked up his encouragement right up until she recognized the tender concern on his face. Maybe Kaylie was right. Maybe he did look at her like he had more than friendly feelings for her.

Or maybe it'd been a fluke, and today's interaction would disprove the theory.

And yet, when he finished studying her class and his attention settled on her, his shoulders relaxed, the crease between his brows disappeared, and finally, his lips turned up.

She hated to admit it, but he looked at her like he cared about her. A lot. Like being in her presence made him happy, even when an entire room kept them from interacting. She finger-combed her hair away from her hot cheeks.

A plump woman in the front row raised a wrinkled hand.

Neenah pounced on the distraction. "Yes?"

"Won't patrolling be dangerous?"

"Observe. Don't ever engage." She resisted looking at Cody. After all, she would've given the warning even without hearing his concerns. "If you see something suspicious, simply report it from a safe distance."

"But at two a.m., what distance is safe?" The question came from the woman's frail-looking friend. "No one would be around to hear my cries for help."

"I hear every other cat fight that happens." The man one row back, Ernie Schilling, ran his thumbs under his suspender straps. "Don't see why I wouldn't hear *you* squawking."

Cody settled back in his chair, smirking.

Neenah held up both hands. "No one should be fighting

or squawking. If you take an overnight shift, please stay in your locked car and perhaps sign up with a friend. Or watch from the window of your house." The last thing she needed was an elderly resident falling in the dead of night with no one to help.

The woman scrawled something on the paper and passed the clipboard to the pair of stay-at-home moms next to her. The two tipped their heads together, apparently conferring on schedules.

"How come all of this is necessary?" one of the few business owners asked. "Isn't this why we pay taxes? To have a police presence?"

At least she'd anticipated this question. "The police have increased patrols, but one thing I love about Redemption Ridge is the way people look out for each other. Having an active neighborhood watch adds an extra layer of security for us all."

The clipboard made its way down the rows. A beefy guy accepted it and scowled down at the form. "I don't know who you think has this much time."

There were a lot of hours in a day, a lot of days in a week. To have round-the-clock coverage, every person in the room would have to sign up for seven hours each week. Unfortunately, the Christmas decorations tended to go missing overnight. The home burglaries happened during the day. Covering only one would leave Redemption Ridge open to the other kind of theft.

"The evening hours from five until ten are the least important," she offered. That was the one window when neither thief had made a move so far. "As many of the other slots we can fill, the better."

Without writing anything, the man shook his head and passed the clipboard along. "I came thinking we could actually do something."

"Watching *is* something." Cody's firm voice caused several residents to turn in their seats. He'd changed out of his uniform, but he still had cop written all over him.

She couldn't have him commanding the room.

She clapped. "Even during uneventful shifts, you get used to the feel of the neighborhood, so you're better prepared to notice when something unusual occurs."

"Like what, dear?" a warbly voice asked.

Neenah had already gone over that—and included the information on the handout—but she repeated a summary of red flags as the clipboard progressed. "And remember, you can always call in suspicious activity, whether it's during your time slot or not. Get used to looking out when you're by a window or if you get up in the night. You never know what you might notice."

As the sole occupant of the last row, Cody received the clipboard and tilted his head to read whatever the others had written.

She wrapped up and her attendees filed out, leaving her, Cody, and her suddenly acrobatic stomach. She collected the informational sheets attendees left behind. That didn't bode well for them following directions when they were on patrol— *if* anyone had signed up.

Cody helped pick up, and when they met in the middle, he passed her the clipboard and paperwork. The schedule gaped woefully empty. Mr. Schilling had volunteered for three a.m. to five a.m. each day. Cody had scrawled his name in the ten to eleven p.m. slot with an asterisk. She turned the clipboard to read his note.

Except when I'm working.

The offer was generous. He already had a full-time job, and no one besides him and the older gentleman had volunteered for a daily shift. The remaining signups combined covered a whopping total of five hours per week.

"Occasional eyes are better than none at all," he said. "And since this is on their minds, they'll be more aware in general."

"Maybe." She covered the signup with the abandoned informational sheets. "Thanks for volunteering. You didn't have to do that."

He shrugged one shoulder. "I wouldn't mind cracking the yeti case. Chief reassigned it to Quince today."

She sucked a breath through her teeth. Did the man have no heart for his son or concern for the community? "I'm sorry. He'll regret that."

Cody scratched his jaw. "Anyway, heard you had an eventful day. What happened with Kaylie and the stop sign?"

"She got upset." She circled back to where she'd left her things. "I saw the stop sign and pointed it out, but she hit the gas instead."

Cody's footsteps followed, and his voice sounded from a few feet behind her. "What was she that upset about?"

Of course he'd immediately ask the one question she didn't want to answer. "What *wasn't* she upset about?"

Cody chuckled and waited.

Neenah pulled on her coat. She couldn't blame the girl. Even teens that hadn't been traumatized weren't known for even-keeled emotions. And since when did she not tell Cody the whole truth? "First, she was nervous to drive with me because I used to be a cop. Even though I explained that doesn't mean I'm there to fault-find."

He nodded as if to say, "Reasonable enough."

"Then she asked why I'm not a cop anymore." She zipped her coat, claimed her belongings from the table, and motioned toward the exit. As he led the way, she continued. "Because of how she responded at dinner the other night when she heard about the neighborhood watch, I steered her away from that one."

He hummed agreement with her decision. "I still have nightmares about that day."

Neenah's step hitched. "Me too."

He acknowledged the admission with a sad smile.

Friendship ought to look this way—open and vulnerable. Supportive.

And since he'd been vulnerable with her, she owed him the same. She confessed the part of the story she'd planned to hold back. "Next, she wanted to know what kind of job I'm looking for, and when I mentioned working security, it was the neighborhood watch discussion all over again. She's convinced something bad will happen, and she was so upset about it, she got flustered and hit the gas."

She pursed her lips and trailed her hand along the wall, waiting for him to side with Kaylie and tell her she needed to work a boring job.

A gust of cold air made her lift her focus from the floor.

Cody held the door for her to step outside. "What are you going to do?"

A question. Not judgment. Not an ultimatum.

"What can I do?" She gave him a grateful smile as she passed outside. "I think the grief group is helpful, so we'll keep going to that."

"Good."

She didn't like needing constant reassurance, but his approval bound up some of the anxiety that had been ricocheting around her chest since the stop sign incident. Yet when he didn't follow it up with a more extensive reply, the worry slipped free again.

They reached her truck.

Cody had parked next to her, but instead of crossing to his vehicle, he lingered. "There is more you can do for Kaylie." He'd measured his words. He clearly didn't think she'd like what he said next.

She unlocked her truck and tossed her belongings inside. Fists balled, she crossed her arms as she turned back to him. "More?"

"I know you don't want to hear it, but if Kaylie's that upset ..." He tipped his head instead of completing the thought.

The implication wrapped around her like a straitjacket. "You think I should get a safer job."

"Only until things settle. Not because you can't handle it, but because she can't."

She studied him. Strong, capable, and confident.

She wanted to fire back a refusal to be limited, a reminder she'd signed up to help a child in need, not to waste her talents.

Cody's confession about nightmares stopped her. She loved Redemption Ridge, but police officers encountered the worst the town had to offer. She'd never heard him mention the traumatic situations giving him nightmares until today. Considering how hard the accident had been on herself and this strong, capable man, could she blame Kaylie for worrying?

She had agreed to help Kaylie. Instead of thinking of surrendering a security job as a waste of her talents, she could consider it an opportunity to lean into different ones and honor her commitment.

"I'm making no promises long term." She winced. Was this really necessary?

Kaylie had released a horrified, high-pitched gasp when she realized she'd blown a stop sign. Then she'd hyperventilated when she saw the flashing lights. Neenah had coached her through breathing exercises while they waited for Garrett to approach, but she'd wished she could do more to spare Kaylie the discomfort.

And now, she could.

For Kaylie's sake, for a couple of weeks, Neenah could

sacrifice a little more. "Piper sounded like she could use help through Christmas."

"Sounds reasonable."

She pointed a finger. "But I'm not giving up the neighborhood watch."

He grinned and turned for his truck. "Never thought for a second you would."

Chapter Eight

The last time Neenah had visited Second Chances, the consignment shop's name, spelled out in mismatched, salvaged letters, matched her mission. She'd needed business casual clothes to get her through desk duty until she rehabilitated her knees and claimed her second chance at serving in uniform. Piper made finding a new wardrobe as painless as possible. And not hard on the bank, either.

As Neenah turned into the lot today, however, her hands nearly shook for how badly she wanted to yank the steering wheel in another direction. Seeking employment here was more like a third chance. An unwanted option that circumstances forced her into taking.

But dwelling on her discontentment wouldn't serve her, Piper, or the customers well.

If she applied herself, she could help others the way she'd once been helped. Since she'd succeeded at learning police procedure, conflict de-escalation, and myriad laws, codes, and ordinances, surely she could gain a passable knowledge of fashion and home furnishing trends. Even if the subjects interested her about as much as eating the cranberry candle Kaylie burned each evening.

She headed for the building. The primary entrance faced Main Street, and the parking lot was tucked behind the row of brick buildings. The back door opened into a hallway. A whiff of paint lurked under the scents of pine and vanilla. The first door she passed in the hall revealed partially completed furniture rehab projects awaiting attention on a drop cloth. She continued past the bathroom and an office.

"Hello!" Piper's cheery greeting drew her toward the edge of the sales floor.

The sales counter stood ahead on the right. Across the room, sunlight streamed through the street-facing windows. To her left, taller clothes racks obscured the view of the fitting rooms. Furniture for sale and table displays filled the center of the space.

"Neenah, what a surprise. What can I help you with?" Piper bustled from behind the counter. "Oh! Do you need Christmas gifts for Kaylie? I just got some cute stuff in." She pivoted for a display.

Neenah shuffled to a stop. She and Cody both hated shopping so much that they went together on most gifts they gave. That way, they each only had to do half the amount of shopping. Or they could go together.

But for her own teenager, Neenah had a special responsibility to come through all on her own. Her dad was a thoughtful gift-giver, which had made the presents her mom mailed all the less enticing as the years went on. After her mom's move, they saw each other less, and she kept picking birthday and Christmas gifts better suited to a younger girl. Kaylie's situation was different, but she deserved well-chosen gifts no less.

Piper passed her a golden picture frame with flowers and vines twining around the exterior. "Maybe she'd like to keep a picture of her mom in a special frame?"

Here she'd expected Piper to start throwing clothes at her. This was a sweeter, more thoughtful gesture. "I'll take it."

Piper flitted to the next table and rummaged through a bowl of jewelry for her next suggestion. In her element, this woman was a cheery whirlwind of ideas.

Still, there'd be plenty of time to learn the inventory and find treasures for Kaylie later, if Neenah ended up working here. But it had been almost a week since Piper made the offer. She might have changed her mind or hired someone else.

Her heart kicked up speed. "I came to see if your offer of a job still stands." Odd how her nerves made it sound as if her voice streamed from somewhere outside her body, a stranger asking for employment at a business where she never imagined herself working.

"Of course." Piper straightened away from the ceramic bowl. "Good help is so hard to find. Were you thinking up front or with the furniture?"

"Up front, if that's all right with you."

"Absolutely. When do you start?"

She laughed. "Isn't that supposed to be up to the boss?"

"I can work around your schedule."

"Kaylie is hanging out with Tori, the runner Bryce introduced her to at the barn dance, so I have time now."

"Perfect." Piper threaded her arm through Neenah's and led her to the office. "A little paperwork, and then we're going to have so much fun."

* * *

Cody pumped a fist. He had a lead on the burglar. Finally.

One Gary Jones, an employee of Tech City, had a record.

Cody grabbed the Tech City employee schedule from a file and laid it over his keyboard. His heel bounced faster each time he confirmed Jones had been working when a burglary victim made a purchase. All three lined up.

He shuffled his papers until he found the schedules for the days burglaries had occurred. Jones had been on shift during two of the thefts. Cody leaned back in his chair, his foot still moving. If the guy left work unexpectedly, that might not show on the printed schedule. Or Jones could've fed information to another party, who committed the burglaries.

The possibility demanded follow-up.

Cody pushed back from his desk and headed for the electronics store. The independent shop occupied one of the larger storefronts downtown. It'd been around as long as he could remember, and based on the seventies-style logo, a couple of decades before then too.

Black walls, a lack of windows, and dim lighting created a dark canvas for the flashing TVs, DJ lights, and stereo displays. Stacks of products and maze-like aisles crowded the sales floor. Shoplifters must have a field day here.

The old building's wood floors creaked beneath his feet as he approached the glass cases that served as a checkout counter.

Clive Robbins, the fifty-something man who managed the store, took off his glasses and rested them on the paperwork he'd been studying. Technically, his build matched the doorbell cam video, but then so did a lot of other men's. "Welcome back, Officer Adams. What can we do for you today?"

"Mr. Robbins." Cody nodded his greeting and scanned the sales floor again. Unless Jones was hunched down behind the closest display, he didn't appear to be in earshot. "I'm here to talk to you about one of your employees. Are you aware Gary Jones was convicted of misdemeanor theft three years ago?"

"What?" Clive's mouth worked silently for a few beats. Finally, he said, "No. We run criminal history checks. That would've come up."

Cody got out his notepad. "When was he hired?"

"Over the summer. I remember because I'd just gotten back from vacation when I interviewed him." As he spoke, Clive angled his head, searching the sales floor. "He's working today. Would you like to talk to him? I'll be forced to let him go now that I'm aware of his record."

Cody spotted movement in an alcove to the side of the store. "Is that him by the speakers?"

"Ah. Yes. Stocking new inventory."

Thanks to the shelves, Cody could only see Jones's dark hair. His height didn't rule him out. "I'll speak with him shortly. First, have you noticed any increase in retail shrink since hiring Mr. Jones?"

"No. If anything, he's noticed and stopped several shoplifters. I've been impressed with his work. I ..." Clive shook his head. "Well, I'm shocked to hear about his record. It's a shame. We're already shorthanded."

"Can you tell me if he completed his full shifts on these dates?" Cody passed the manager a list of the days Jones had been working while a burglary occurred.

"That will require the computer in the office. I'd rather not leave the register with a thief, but I suppose we've made it this long. His till is usually accurate, and the evening manager should report for his shift any minute now." Clive called for Jones to man the register.

The twenty-something's pale skin contrasted with his almost-black hair, and he dressed like Cody's high school math teacher had—brown leather slip-on shoes, khaki pants, plaid button-down. His light-green eyes flicked to Cody and then away, as if the impression of a uniform was enough information. He kept his chin down as he took his boss's place behind the register.

He hadn't run on the spot, but he might make a break for it when Cody stepped away. He followed Clive only as far as the office door so he could watch for any sudden dash to the exit.

A few minutes later, Clive tilted his head to see through the bottom of his bifocals. He clicked another key, then nodded. "He did complete his full shifts. Both days."

"How about breaks?"

"He clocked out for half-hour unpaid breaks."

"Times?"

Clive maneuvered from one week's schedule to the other and listed them. The first fell within the window of the burglary in question, but that was a span of several hours. The second break didn't match the more exact time they had for the last theft.

Cody jotted the times on his notepad. "Is there any way an employee could leave during their shift without someone noticing?"

Clive paused thoughtfully. "We offer installation services. I suppose if he was installing a car stereo, he could leave the garage without the employee inside realizing it."

Movement in his periphery caught Cody's attention. A man approached the office, a backpack slung over one shoulder. In jeans and a zip-up hoody, he didn't exude authority, but Clive introduced him as Zane Harris, the evening manager.

Zane side-eyed Cody. "Everything okay?"

"Gary has a record," Clive groused.

Furrows appeared across the younger man's forehead. "But you knew that. I left the background check with his application. I was surprised when you offered him the job anyway, but I figured you believed him."

Clive sputtered, worked a set of keys from his pocket, and reached for a file cabinet drawer. "Believed him about what?"

"To hear him tell it, he's innocent."

"If a judge didn't believe him, I'm not going to." Clive plucked a manilla folder from the drawer and plopped it open on the desk. He paged through papers for a hurried moment, then sat back in his chair with a grunt.

A report showing Gary Jones's offense lay beside the application.

"I did everything just like normal." Zane tapped a pointed finger next to a check mark on the application. "I checked the box that I ran the report, and then since he had a record, I attached the report to the application."

He'd done so with a paper clip. Not the most secure method.

"It wasn't there when I did the interview."

Cody watched them carefully. An oversight like this could indicate something more complicated was going on. One of the managers might be involved. If so, Jones might be an accomplice or simply a fall guy. Or it was all coincidence. "Who had access to the file?"

Clive released a long exhale, and his focus wandered the desk. "Applications sometimes sit in a file on the desk. Any employee who came through at the right time might've tampered with it. We've never had issues like this. This is just a small-town store."

Zane's mouth tightened into a frown.

Both managers looked more embarrassed than deceitful, but looks could be misleading. He would check their schedules against the thefts.

He made a few more notes before turning the interview back to his earlier line of questions. "You mentioned a garage where employees might leave without being noticed. Are there cameras there?"

Clive shook his head. "Only in the store, and between us, the only one that works is the one on the main door."

"Did Jones complete an install on any of the days in question?"

Clive checked his watch. "Zane, can you review the receipts? I have to pick up my son."

"Yeah, okay." The younger manager hung his backpack from a hook and took his boss's place at the computer. "This'll take a bit."

Cody left him to the task and approached the checkout. "Gary Jones?"

"Yes?" He pushed his horn-rimmed glasses up the bridge of his nose.

"Have you heard about the string of home burglaries?"

Jones scratched his neck. "I guess I heard about one. There's more?"

"Three so far, all Tech City customers."

"Oh. Hm. Well ..." The guy shoved his hands in his pockets and pressed his mouth shut.

"The first one occurred on November nineteenth. Can I ask where you were that day?"

His eyes bugged. "You think I did it?"

"I'd like to rule you out. I'm aware of your record."

He shot a glance at the office door and lowered his voice. "Man, like, that was all a misunderstanding."

Yet he'd pled guilty. "You can understand why I need to ask a few questions so we can keep you out of the current situation as much as possible." He nodded to Clive as the man passed and exited.

Jones waited until the door shut behind him and hissed, "You gotta tell my bosses I didn't rob anybody. Not now, not before."

"What were you doing on November nineteenth?"

Chewing his lip, Jones consulted his phone. "I was home. My roommates saw me there."

"Were they with you between nine a.m. and two p.m.?"

"Yeah. On and off."

"You were alone at some point?"

"Well, yeah. But that doesn't make me a criminal."

"Can I get your roommates' names and phone numbers?" They wouldn't be much use for clearing Jones, but they might be accomplices or aware of suspicious behavior.

By the time he wrapped up the interview, Zane returned with news that there had been no installations on the days in question.

As Jones returned to stocking shelves, Zane dropped his tone. "You know, there's another possibility besides installs. Gary is sometimes assigned tasks in the stockroom, where he's out of sight for an hour or more at a stretch."

"Can you show me the stockroom?"

"It's through there." Zane motioned toward a door. "You can look around. The store has nothing to hide, and if you're done with him, I'm supposed to send Gary packing."

Cody visited the stockroom, found a door at the back, and passed into a two-stall garage, presumably where they did stereo installations. The grimy window looked out on his cruiser in the lot. As he'd been warned, he could leave from here without anyone on the sales floor noticing.

His phone buzzed, and he paused in the privacy of the garage to answer.

"Got another burglary," Justin reported. "Same MO. Another Tech City customer."

"When did it happen? Exactly?"

"Home owner has cameras, so you're in luck... According to the time stamps, a white truck pulled into the driveway thirty-eight minutes ago. One minute later, the burglar covered the camera before it recorded anything else. At that point, the homeowner called us. First officer rolled up on the scene five minutes later, and the burglar was already gone."

The whole thing happened before Cody arrived at the store. He pinned his phone to his ear with his shoulder and took his pen to his notepad. "Address?"

Justin read it off.

Cody jotted it down and frowned. "How long you think it'd take to drive from there to Tech City?"

"Seven, maybe eight minutes?"

Cody tapped the end of his pen on the paper. Given what he'd learned about the ease with which employees could sneak out, no one had an alibi. Clive hadn't seemed to know where Jones was when Cody first asked after him, after all. And then there was Zane, whose shift just started ten minutes ago.

He ended the call, went back in, and asked to see the afternoon's transaction information. Jones's name appeared on a transaction three minutes after the latest burglary started.

"Thing is..." Zane winced. "If Gary was the one logged into the register and the manager on duty just happened to help one person, he might've just rung it up under Gary."

Cody's eyes sank closed. Did this store observe no firm policies? Employees could sneak out at will, the register information may or may not be accurate, and background checks could randomly disappear.

"I mean, we're not supposed to. I'm just saying, things happen. You could ask Clive about it. I'm sure he'd be honest if that's what he did here."

Right. The burglar had been wise to pick this store as a way to find targets. Information and alibies were as hole-ridden as a grade-school snowflake cutout. "Where were you during the hour leading up to your shift today?"

Zane's eyes widened. "I, uh, went for a run, showered, and came in."

"Anyone see you?"

"Someone, probably, while I was running. Back at home, no. I live alone."

Of course he did. Because no one could have a firm alibi.

Cody took his leave. Praying the Lord would give him a break, he strolled the parking lot and looked in the windows of the handful of parked vehicles. He found no white truck, and no backseat loaded with electronics. He pulled out of the lot, no closer to closing his case than when he'd arrived.

Chapter Nine

Each Redemption Ridge Christmas tradition Kaylie heard about became her new favorite, or so she said, possibly because Neenah kept caving when she made the claim. Tonight's activity? The annual cookie decorating contest. The tradition marked one week until Christmas, and Neenah had attended for years—as a spectator.

Kaylie, however, wasn't the type to sit on the sidelines.

"I really don't want to compete." Neenah lifted her voice over the exultant strains of "Deck the Halls," Kaylie's choice for their drive to the contest.

"But it's going to be so fun. And I loved the cookies you decorated back at our house."

She'd loved *laughing* at them, maybe. Neenah didn't bother to look over because not even her best cop glare would win this fight for her. She didn't want to win by intimidation anyway. Not when she was working so hard to ensure Kaylie remained as happy and engaged with life as possible.

Kaylie had been relieved when Neenah announced her new job at Second Chances. And after a little over a week of shifts, Neenah was catching on to how the shop worked.

Horse therapy and running together continued to go well, although they still had their moments too. Kaylie never liked it when Neenah took a neighborhood watch shift, for example. And something reminded her of her mom every day. But they'd kept their heads above water.

Declining to compete in the decorating contest wouldn't sink them, so long as Neenah found a kind way to bow out. "As I recall, you took one of those cookies of mine and posted a whole series of pictures of it."

With glee, Kaylie had drawn different backdrops for the poorly decorated cookie. By placing the cookie in a different position on each one, she'd made the single confection resemble a dozen different subjects. "It takes talent to decorate a polar bear so it could also be a seal or a yogi or a koala bear or—"

Fighting a grin, Neenah sliced a hand through the air to cut her off. "You'll have to find someone else to team up with. Just don't expect an easy win. People around here get pretty competitive, and usually, a couple of professionals enter."

"That seems like cheating."

"It's the game they all play. So my polar koala seal and I will be sitting this one out."

"Fine." Kaylie huffed playfully. "Do you think Tori will be there? Maybe she'll team up with me."

"We'll have to see." Usually partnerships formed before the event started, though, so she wasn't surprised when Tori and Bryce were both already committed to teams.

The tables at the center of the room, where she and Cody sat each year to watch and snack and talk, drew Neenah. Cody hadn't arrived yet, but Piper claimed a table with her kids. Graham occupied a competitor's station, teamed up with Piper's grandma.

"Oh!" Kaylie bounded away.

Neenah spun to see who she'd set her sights on as her next potential recruit.

Cody had barely made it through the door. He wore his jacket open over a dark-blue crew neck she'd bet her last Christmas cookie was his Redemption Ridge PD T-shirt. He stopped short when he spotted Kaylie charging up and a slow smile tugged his lips. Her enthusiasm was a sight to behold.

The girl let out a gush of words Neenah couldn't hear over the conversations around her, but the clasped hands and pleading eyes conveyed the meaning.

Based on the other night, Cody's decorating skills didn't much surpass Neenah's. Yet his full smile broadcast his response before he nodded. Only then did his blue eyes seek Neenah out, lips still upturned.

When all that handsome happiness focused on her, her breath whooshed from her lungs like Santa Claus disappearing up a chimney.

She never should've become best friends with someone who could take her breath away like that. Every glance they shared made her wish relationships did last and living happily ever after would be as easy as letting their friendship grow into more.

Yet Kaylie needed someone to step up, not only for the contest but also as a male role model. A swell of gratitude for his willingness had her mouthing her thanks. He nodded back and followed Kaylie. Neenah caught herself staring after him and pulled herself away to join Piper and the kids.

In a carrier beside her mother, Opal jiggled a set of plastic keys. Meanwhile, Jasper sat on Piper's lap, shading in a cartoon elf. An assortment of coloring pages and crayons waited on the table.

Piper braced the page for her son as she tipped her head toward Kaylie and Cody. "How do you think they'll do?"

"We made sugar cookies the other night. He decorated

each one in a solid color. Kaylie is artistic, though. She might save them from getting laughed out of here." Neenah scanned the competitors. Probably the best match for their skill level was Hollis and Lucy Price, back from rodeo finals. Bryce and his buddy might do worse. Most of the others would likely produce better results.

Movement drew her attention as Will Price, Hollis's brother, approached. "Is this the eating table?"

"Sure is." Neenah motioned to an open chair.

The cowboy dropped into it. The Price brothers bore a strong resemblance to each other, both a similar height with lean, work-toughened builds and reddish-brown hair, but in contrast to Hollis's sharp features, Will's were more rounded. Tonight, he wore a sweatshirt, jeans, and foam clogs. Hard to believe he'd recently come from competing in the National Finals Rodeo with Hollis.

"How was NFR?" she asked.

His trademark grin overtook his face. "We won a few rounds and placed second in the average. We're happy, considering it was our first year back after focusing on the ranch."

Piper picked up a crayon and started filling in the elf hat. "I heard you met someone."

Will snagged a coloring page and a red crayon. He didn't answer, but the blush on his cheeks suggested there was some truth to the rumor.

"She's a barrel racer," Piper supplied. "She's coming to look at a horse in a few weeks, and my bet is, she never leaves."

Will scoffed and shook his head. "You are a hopeless romantic."

"Says the guy coloring in a kissing Mr. and Mrs. Claus." Piper pointed with her crayon toward his coloring sheet.

Will leaned back and cocked his head as if he hadn't bothered to notice the design before laying down color. The rotund couple did indeed lean toward each other with lips puckered while Santa held mistletoe above their heads.

Jasper pulled a face. "Ew."

Will shrugged it off and resumed his doodling.

"I hear you two hit it off," Piper continued. "Since you built that new house out on the ranch, maybe it's time for the next step in life."

Neenah suppressed a sigh. She'd had her own home longer than Will, but she hadn't taken any next steps. Until recently, next steps hadn't interested her. She'd been content with her career and her horse. And now...

Cody shed his jacket and donned an apron. The RRPD logo on his T-shirt showed around the apron strings. Judging by his intense focus on the cookies and supplies, he wanted to memorize whatever instructions Kaylie was dictating.

"I think you're skipping a couple of steps in between meeting and marrying." Will turned his page for a better angle. "Ashley's great, but even I'm not making a lifetime commitment after two weeks."

"I'm not saying you should get married immediately," Piper said. "But there's got to be a happy medium between love at first sight and ten plus years of mutual pining."

What an awfully specific example. Neenah's gaze cut over. Piper lifted her eyebrows in feigned innocence. Graham must never have shared with his wife the signs of deception they'd been trained to watch for in interrogations.

Will looked between Piper and Neenah, then shook his head and got back to coloring.

Neenah quit resisting the sigh. Her line of sight wandered to Cody. Again.

Together, they could find out where this rollercoaster ride would lead.

Except... if all went well, this rollercoaster of attraction could lead to marriage and children, and was she in a place to keep lifelong promises like those?

Cody stuck his tongue out in concentration as he outlined the top of a cookie, then filled the space with icing. Beside him, Kaylie set aside a finished cookie and then checked his progress. Her mouth dropped open in dismay, and she waved him to move faster.

Neenah couldn't hear his response, but he continued at a snail's pace. He might not be the best cookie competition partner, but observant and attentive, he'd make a good husband and father. If only Neenah could cut it as a wife and mother, but she'd already taken the biggest risk she could by taking in Kaylie. If she made vows to Cody, started a family, and then failed them, she'd never forgive herself.

* * *

In the same way that coffee helped kick off his mornings, Cody's hour-long neighborhood watch shifts became his preferred routine to wind down each day. Cruising the sleepy streets of Redemption Ridge with music streaming from his speakers and no traffic violations or paperwork to worry about allowed him to decompress, pray, and feel more useful than when he sat on his couch catching up on games he'd missed.

He valued those benefits even more than he otherwise would have, thanks to the burglary case.

Gary Jones's roommates let him do a walk-through, but he found no stash of stolen electronics and no white pickup. Jones himself pulled up partway through, driving an old sedan with a muffler so loud, Cody warned him to fix it. No way that vehicle could sneak around town stealing things without everyone noticing.

Meanwhile, Zane and Clive answered all of his questions. While he couldn't clear them, nothing pointed strongly to their involvement. Interviewing other store employees also yielded nothing helpful.

Between trying to predict the culprit's next move, investigating each occurrence as though it might be its own case, and following up on tips from well-meaning citizens, he'd spent a lot of time getting nowhere.

He forced a deep breath. The beauty of neighborhood watch shifts was not obsessing about any of that. He turned the mystery over to God, as he'd had to do daily to get any peace of mind, and reversed his truck down his driveway.

A flash of movement—a person—in the backup camera made him mash the brake. He craned his neck to get eyes on whoever had jogged across his vehicle's path.

Sure would be an awesome blessing if he'd surprised the burglar or the yeti while backing out of his own driveway. He reached for his seatbelt, ready to give chase, but then a head bobbed outside the passenger window. Too short to be the burglar. Dark hair instead of a white yeti costume.

The person knocked on the window and yanked open the door. The dome light illuminated Neenah's grin. Her eyes sparkled as she took him in with a glance, then she laughed. "Spooked?"

"Watchful." He let go of the seat buckle, loosened his grip on the steering wheel, and kept his tone even to disguise the familiar delight her presence always stirred in him. "That *is* the idea of a neighborhood watch."

Neenah hopped into the passenger seat. As she shut the door, the dome light went off again, cloaking them in comfortable darkness.

"Going somewhere?" His chiding tone grated against the pleasure swelling in his chest, but he wasn't about to scare her off with too warm a welcome. To ensure she couldn't make a run for it, he let off the brake.

She buckled in. "I've got an hour to spare."

"Where's Kaylie?"

"Home. She's old enough. Besides, neither she nor I have shopped at Tech City in over a year, and my phone will go off if the security cameras pick up movement in the yard." Neenah settled deeper into her seat. "Figured keeping you company's the least I could do after you made Kaylie's cookie decorating dreams come true."

He pulled onto the road. "I highly doubt any dreams were realized tonight."

Neenah didn't respond. Or had she, but quietly enough for the low tones of the music to cover her voice? The volume control glowed on the dash, but turning it down might call attention to how much he valued what she had to say.

Considering how long he'd been hiding his feelings, this game should be second nature. Still wasn't.

They passed a streetlight. In the glow, Neenah's eyebrows lifted. "She narrated a blow-by-blow replay of the whole night. I might as well have been seated right between you the entire time."

Her presence would've been a nice addition. For himself anyway. Kaylie would've had a fit if he'd gone any slower, though, and from what Neenah said, she'd never had a father figure at all. Stepping up was worth a little sacrifice of time with Neenah. Especially since she'd given him the opportunity to make it up now.

"I'm glad she enjoyed herself. That was the plan." Head-lights loomed not far behind his tailgate, and he pulled over, allowing the car to pass before he resumed his slow pass down the street.

"Did your parents do that for you?"

"Huh?"

Shadows cloaked her face. "Did they do things for you just because you'd enjoy them back in high school?"

He clenched his teeth and resumed scanning front yards

and driveways. How was he supposed to notice a new absence of decorations when she was probing into his childhood dynamics with his parents? "My mom did. And life was different for me. I had friends. Kaylie had to move away from hers."

"When's the last time you remember your dad doing something for you?" She might as well have found a tack and pressed it into his chest.

With anyone else, he'd change the subject, but this was Neenah. She could ask for a kidney, and he'd be on the phone scheduling surgery. He could answer a simple question. "He's giving me a shot at detective."

"You earned that." The snap in her tone meant she wanted better for him. That pushed the tack deeper, because the paltry offering was all his dad had given him. "Considering he's not exactly cheering for you, it's hardly a gift."

He scratched his chest but couldn't dislodge the sharp ache. No use hiding the fact that they were having a serious conversation when she was the one who'd taken things that direction. He spun the knob, and the sound faded. "What are you getting at?" He cut her a look.

Neenah massaged her palm with her thumb. "Watching you with Kaylie showed how different you are from him."

Finally, the tack eased back half a millimeter. He turned onto Main Street. "You just noticed the differences between me and Chief now?"

"It's not that." Her sigh breezed over the hum of the truck. "But I am inspired by it now."

He was as honored as he was confused. "Your dad's great, isn't he?"

"Sure, but my mom wasn't."

"Okay ..." He'd meant the prompt to keep her talking, but she quieted.

The giant community Christmas tree twinkled in the

town square. Lights illuminated garlands and ribbons on the streetlights along Main. At least he could rule out the yeti upping his game and packing up everything on Main Street.

He turned into a residential area. Though he never drove the same route twice, he'd been through often enough to know what to expect. The house two doors down had a projector that cast pinpricks of light like stars all over a large, bare oak. Cody slowed to look up at the branches. If he let the silence stretch, especially if they crawled along so there wasn't much entertainment out the windows either, Neenah might fill the void with an explanation.

After the galaxy tree, he swung his attention across the street to the light-up sleigh and reindeer. The house next door had lights strung from the eaves and down the corners. All evidence the yeti hadn't been through.

Someone had, however, stolen Neenah's words.

He tried prompting her. "You're not going to abandon Kaylie, if that's what this is about."

"Right. Yeah. Kaylie's only going to need me to be heavily involved a couple of years. I can do that."

Then he had no idea why she needed inspiration to believe she could overcome her mother's legacy. He wound his way through the neighborhood. Movement made him stop once, but the culprit turned out to be a cat. He moved on.

"What do you think makes a couple change their minds and divorce after years of marriage and four kids?" The soft question almost drowned under road noise and the whisper of music.

What was he supposed to say? She'd rarely talked about her parents' split. He had no idea why the family had fractured.

Neenah continued in the same quiet tone. "I've always kind of figured it was a problem that was there all along and grew too big to ignore. That's how Dad made it sound. But every relationship has little problems. That's why I've never dated anyone for long. I don't know how to tell which little red flags are going to stay little and which will eventually turn into deal breakers. So I just ..." She clicked her tongue and made a slicing motion with her hand.

"That's not what you told me." The words were out before he could think better of them. When he'd asked her out and she'd shot him down, she'd warned him that broaching the subject again would spell the end for their friendship. That possibility filled the cab until it became stuffy and hard to breathe. He might be safe, though. She'd brought up the subject. He was just seeing it through. "You said you were focused on your career."

"I focused on my career because I haven't been able to figure out why some marriages last and others don't. Joke's on me. It turns out careers are the same. Some last, others don't. Do you think marriages are equally beyond our control?"

He wanted to argue that two committed people could control the outcome. But that was only true if both did, indeed, stay committed, and no one could force a spouse to keep wedding vows. Plus, accidents or illness could take a spouse too. "Outcomes are out of our control but under our influence."

Neenah made a soft sound in her throat, a hum of deep thought.

Cody stared into the night that surrounded them. He and Neenah had discussed life and death, healing and pain, justice and mercy, but never romance or marriage. Except the time he'd asked her out and she'd shut him down, but that hardly qualified as a discussion. Yet she'd steered the conversation this direction, and she wasn't cutting it off. She had to be considering a relationship with someone.

Him?

Someone else?

She had visited with Will Price during the cookie competition. The rodeo star might've needed only an hour of conversation to rope a woman's heart. Especially considering Neenah's penchant for quick decisions. But this was Neenah. *His* Neenah. He wouldn't go down without a fight. If this was his one chance to tell her what he'd be to her if only she'd allow him, he refused to pass it up.

"Habits have to back up vows. Take my vow to protect and serve the community. To make sure I follow through, I complete training, practice at the gun range, and stay in shape. One day, when I make my marriage vows, my habits are going to back them up. And the good news for my wife is that they won't be new habits. I'm already following Jesus, staying accountable to believing friends, even seeing a counselor once in a while."

Neenah chuckled. "Like when you're forced to because of a work incident."

His mouth went dry. He'd allowed that misunderstanding to go on too long. "The counselor I saw after your injury wasn't mandatory. I chose to go." Much to his dad's chagrin. "Letting you get hurt was eating me up."

"You didn't *let* that happen. We were both doing our jobs that day. Neither of us had any way to predict how it would go."

He inhaled until he felt the stretch in his chest. "Jim—the counselor—asked me to imagine what it would've been like to know in advance what would happen, what you would've said if I'd tried to keep you from covering the back while I was in front. Every time I pictured it, you charged ahead with the original plan anyway. Jim reminded me you'd sworn to the same things as me, and I didn't get to try to stop you from keeping your promises."

"Well." Her tone turned wry. "If I'd known about the car,

I would've stayed out of its path. Or gone faster to cut them off before they reached the vehicle."

"But you still would've gone, even knowing the danger."

"Yes."

A quiet block passed. Cody turned back toward Main Street so he could cross to another neighborhood. "As terrible as it's been, I hope that entire situation puts you at ease about your ability to follow through on your side of a marriage. Not only could nothing have prevented you from doing your job that day, but you also pursued rehabilitation and reinstatement until it wasn't possible to continue." He stopped for the intersection by the town square.

Surprise, surprise, no traffic. Just another dark and normal night in Redemption Ridge.

He eased into the intersection. "You don't have to fear being someone who gives up too easily. If I trust anyone to see a commitment through to the bitter end, it's you."

The statement was loaded. A few minutes ago, he'd promised to keep his end of a marriage. Now, he'd given his strongest vote of confidence in Neenah's ability to do so as well. He'd painted a picture of what their future together could look like, Lord and Neenah willing. If she recognized as much, she might keep her promise to sever ties.

He slipped his thumb under his seatbelt and adjusted how it lay. Still felt like a barbell had fallen across his chest with crushing weight.

"The yeti struck again." She pointed through the windshield.

"What?" He forced his focus to the square. Dark and normal, just as he'd concluded moments before.

But this wasn't the season of darkness. It was the season of lights. The community Christmas tree, which had been aglow minutes before, had become a hulking shadow.

Chapter Ten

Neenah's breath rushed, shallow and hurried, and not because of any exertion as she circled the massive Christmas tree for clues. Cody was one of the most important people in her life, and she couldn't say when that had happened. She could, however, pinpoint the moment when a longing for a very different future with him had powerfully and undeniably taken root.

It'd been when he referred to his *wife*.

Scorching jealousy had spilled from head to toe like hot tar that clung to her still.

She'd tried to make light of it by picking on him for what he said about seeing a counselor. The low blow hadn't distracted her. Her feelings weren't surface-level fluff. Rather, like a sapling growing unnoticed, her attraction to him had developed deep roots she couldn't simply pull out with her bare hands.

And if his speech about their abilities to commit proved true, she didn't have to.

"Think we're dealing with more than one person?" Cody

rounded the tree and stopped beside her, neck craned as he looked up at the branches.

After all these years, she couldn't simply tell him she'd changed her mind.

Could she?

Even considering it felt like taking a stray step off a rooftop.

She focused on the task before her.

Some ornaments, perfectly round, nested amidst the irregular shape of the boughs. Others had fallen and lay scattered across the ground like escapees from a child's ball pit. Beneath, visitors' boots had packed the ground, so no distinguishable footprints offered clues. A ring of coal circled the base of the tree, however, suggesting the yeti's involvement.

"They worked fast," Cody said. "This was lit up when we first passed."

"It may have been partially undone when we came through."

"Possible. And undoing lights must go faster than putting them up."

Excellent point—one that perhaps also applied to the boundaries she'd built between them.

Cody thunked an ornament with the toe of his boot, and it bounced into the nearest piece of coal. "Especially if you don't care what you break."

Therein lay the problem. She did care if she broke something between herself and Cody.

But they'd survived her turning him down years ago. It would only be fair for him to forgive her for bringing it up once herself. Besides, Cody had spoken openly about marriage and commitment in the truck. She ought to be able to take the conversation a little further without doing serious damage.

Her heart ran in place like a 1980s aerobics instructor.

The only thing left to do was to say it.

Maybe I was wrong.

About what? he'd ask.

Turning you down, back when you asked me out.

And then he'd be pleased or uncomfortable, but either way, she'd have opened the door.

"Maybe—"

"This is Cody Adams." He had his phone to his ear. How had she missed him dialing? "I'm off duty but came across what looks to be another Christmas decoration theft."

He must've called the police station. While reporting the crime was the appropriate next step, any declarations of interest on her part would have to wait until after an officer came for their statement. At that point, it'd be even later, and she really ought to get home to Kaylie.

Her feelings would have to take a rain check.

As he finished his call, Cody's voice rumbled confident and low, and his posture conveyed strength, but the night dimmed his features. His blond hair and eyebrows were only faintly distinguishable from his skin, and shadows cloaked his blue eyes.

Neither of them would be able to read the other's expression well. That meant they'd have something of a buffer if she did go ahead and blurt it out. Then, being forced to go their separate ways shortly afterward would give them time to process.

Maybe now was ideal.

Cody returned his phone to his pocket. "Should only be a few minutes. Garrett's on duty tonight, and he's nearby. I wonder if they'll—"

"I like how you interacted with Kaylie."

His face swung toward her. The shift revealed a streetlight beyond him, and in contrast, his expression became even more unreadable. Silence stretched.

The plan had already gone awry. She hadn't intended to

cut him off or bring up Kaylie—again. Now, if she brought up dating, it'd sound like an idea borne from desperation to secure help with her new ward.

"Thanks," he said.

"You, um ..." She cleared her throat. "Still want kids of your own someday?"

After bringing up Kaylie, what else could she say?

He cocked his head. "Yes."

"I think you'll be a great father."

He didn't reply. The absence of a thank you only under-scored how awkward this had gotten.

Time to correct course. She pivoted toward the tree again. "You wonder if they'll ... what?"

"Huh?"

"I interrupted you. You were wondering about if someone would do something. I assume 'they' is the station."

Cody took a beat. "I wonder if they'll get Quince up. It's his case."

"But it's not a particularly urgent one."

"True." His voice dragged like an anchor stuck on her awkward interjection.

"We should do another pass. If we can break open the case, you'll get the promotion." She stepped away. The town square's electrical box had to be somewhere. Cody might've already stopped there, but a second look couldn't hurt.

"Neenah." His voice was stern.

Her heart scurried up her throat. She turned to face him.

"You're acting weird."

"How so?"

Headlights turned onto the street. With any luck, it'd be Garrett, there to interrupt. Instead, the vehicle cruised by without stopping. She pulled her attention from the taillights back to Cody.

He remained squared off to her. "You showed up unannounced. You brought up marriage and commitment and parenthood." He crossed his arms. "You asked if I want kids like my answer would affect you."

"Of course it would. We're best friends. Anything in your life affects mine."

"This game …" He narrowed his eyes and frowned. Second thoughts about what he was saying, perhaps? "Is an insult to your intelligence and mine."

Neenah shoved her hands in her coat pockets. When the man was right, he was right. "Maybe. It wouldn't be the first time I made a bad decision."

There. She'd botched the script, but she'd announced that she regretted a past decision. Sort of.

He balled his fists and crossed his arms, but the movement looked more self-protective than offended.

Ugh. She didn't operate like this, all wishy-washy and indirect. She made decisions, saw them through, and dealt with the consequences as they came. She plunged headlong into the truth. "I was wrong to put my career first. I think, like you said, I was wrong about my ability to commit to a relationship. And perhaps together, we could've gotten your dad on our side. So, when you asked me out, I should've said yes."

Cody's hands dropped to his sides. His lips parted.

"Howdy, folks." Garrett's greeting might as well have been a PIT maneuver for the way it spun her around both mentally and figuratively.

Her sudden whirl toward him widened Garrett's eyes, and he gave a helpless smile. "You witnessed a crime?"

"We didn't witness it." Cody's steady voice suggested he'd seen Garrett approaching. Yet he'd kept Neenah talking. "We *did* notice the effects."

As he recited what they knew, including the times when they'd last seen the lights and first noticed them missing. Neenah replayed her confession.

When you asked me out, I should've said yes.

Her statement had been past tense and hadn't specified her present desire to rectify her mistake. She'd spent so long leaving her affections out of the conversation that she'd forgotten how to speak up about them. She could change tactics and swap in action for talking. Marching up and kissing him would send a clear message.

Her whole face tingled at the thought. It'd been years since she'd kissed a man. She remembered it being ... fun, but only when the moment came as a natural extension of the relationship. Was kissing a natural next step with her best friend?

Even standing beside him in the shadowy park, she could recall all the details of his face. Cody had a strong chin and a bottom lip that was more pronounced than the top one. He didn't have dimples, but the lines bracketing his smile showed faintly even when he wasn't smiling because of how often he used them. If she touched his jaw at this hour, she'd feel the grit of stubble and, if her fingers rested high enough by his ear, the soft bristle of his hair, which was buzzed on the sides and combed into a neat style on top.

Once or twice after he'd adopted the conservative and gelled style, she'd ruffled it up. He'd ducked and swatted her hands away, complaining. But she'd bet she could get away with mussing it up during a kiss.

"Neenah, do you have anything to add?" Garrett asked.

Good thing he'd used her name, or she wouldn't have heard the question. As it was, she had no idea if she'd noticed a detail Cody hadn't because she'd missed his statement. It was unlikely, though. Even off duty, the man was good at his job. Focused.

Something she no longer seemed to be.

Perhaps she—and Chief Adams—had been right all along that romance and police work didn't mix.

* * *

Cody watched Neenah beeline for a truck the same color and model as her own. She must be flustered if she'd forgotten she hadn't driven herself to the square. When her keys, which he assumed were in her pocket, didn't unlock the vehicle, she'd realize her blunder. He spared her the embarrassment of calling her out and got behind the wheel of his own ride.

Twenty seconds later, she climbed into the passenger seat. "Not a word," she grumbled.

He chuckled. "Are you sure you want to swear me to silence on another subject when you're already regretting the first one?"

She went still. Here he'd thought she'd be relieved he broke the ice that had formed when Garrett interrupted.

He started the truck, pulled into the driving lane, and tried another tack. "What did you mean when you said that together, we could've gotten my dad on our side? What made you think Chief was against us to begin with?"

Neenah smoothed her hair. "I shouldn't have mentioned that."

"But you did. Explain."

"It's nothing. He just ..." She shook her head and exhaled forcefully. "Doesn't like his officers to date each other."

Neenah wouldn't have been dissuaded by an abstract suggestion of disapproval. Suspicion wound through the tendons of his neck. "What did he say?"

"Nothing ... recently."

The suspicion hardened to steel, and a headache threatened. "And years ago?"

"Remember how I told you I knew he wanted you to be police chief someday yourself?"

"Yes."

"I knew because he told me."

"How is that related to you and me?" His arms and abs tensed, ready for the blow of her next words.

They didn't come.

Neenah gripped the armrest and bit her lips together. Classic signs of a witness holding back.

Cody would have to fill in the blanks based on what he knew of his father. Which, unfortunately, provided enough background to make an educated guess. "He told you neither of our careers would go anywhere if we were to date."

"Yes."

Anger grayed his vision, and he narrowed his eyes to focus on the road. They'd made it a few blocks closer to his house before he asked, "When was this?"

"Four years ago."

"Four years." Four wasted years. Four years they could've been happy together.

"Four and a half," Neenah specified.

"Right before I asked you out?" It made sense. His dad had spoken with him around the same time, discouraging any romantic attachment with Neenah. How his old man had seen the signs, Cody didn't know, but he was a police officer at heart. He noticed details, acted on hunches. Although given this latest information, his dad applied those skills less like a police officer and more like a conniving movie villain.

"I would've said no anyway." Neenah's voice was as quick as the swipe of a broom, swishing the mess beneath a rug. "I had already concluded I was better off focusing on my work. I didn't ... well, my parents calling it quits so many years in scared me. Made me wonder if I could trust anyone—myself included—to stay committed for the long haul. I figured career advancement was better than heartbreak, so that's where I focused. But turns out a career can break your heart, too, and maybe none of us are as doomed to repeat our parents' mistakes as I thought."

She made it sound so cut-and-dried, as if she'd sworn off all men long before Chief intervened when he knew that wasn't the case. "You used to date some."

"Well ... yeah."

"Something pushed you over the edge to ruling it out entirely."

"We can't blame your dad for that. He was involved, but it was ... it was actually a relief to have that off the table, because I did think about dating you, but I was torn because we were also good friends, and if we tried more and it didn't work out, I would be missing both my best friend and my boyfriend. It seemed a lot smarter to stick with the option where I got to keep my friend and safeguard both of our careers. Although, for wanting you to advance so far, he sure has been slow about promoting you."

"My career was never more important to me than you."

That had been too forward. Too much. His lungs froze.

He glanced over, trying to read her expression.

She tipped her face down until her hair—loose for once—shielded it from view.

Why had he restarted this conversation in a vehicle? They ought to be face-to-face, where they could benefit from reading each other's facial expressions and body language. This was a dangerous conversation to navigate with such limited visibility. He vowed to hold his peace until they reached his house.

"You came before my career too." The hum of the vehicle almost drowned out her soft-spoken words. "That's why I never would've traded places with you the day I got hurt."

He nodded to accept the statement, but he kept his promise to himself and waited to finish the conversation. After all, he'd been waiting for years. What was another few blocks?

His leg jiggled. A few more blocks turned into torture.

He parked in his driveway and turned to Neenah, but she got out and headed for her truck.

"Can we finish this conversation?" he called after her.

She turned slowly. "You want to?"

"Yes. Of course." He extended his hand toward his house.

She dropped her gaze and passed inside. The back entrance opened into the space between his kitchen and dining room. He'd purchased the dining table and chairs from a bona fide furniture store for a lot of money, mostly because his parents had made a big deal about their table when he'd grown up. The acquisition had seemed like a sign of success, but with no one to keep him company at it most nights, he'd soon given up eating there. He either ate out with friends or in front of his TV with a game playing.

Now, however, he motioned to the closest seat at the table.

Probably should've offered to take her coat first, but the black leather jacket suited her. Her athleticism showed in the fit of her clothes, the upright posture as she sat.

She looked good there, in his home and at his table. Did he dare believe she'd styled her silky hair down for his benefit?

Without bothering to shed his own coat, he claimed the chair beside hers, their knees nearly touching.

She picked at her fingernails. "When you asked me out, I should've said yes."

So she'd said, but he wasn't tired of hearing the words. Her regret about her original answer could mean she'd offer a new one now. Except she chewed her lip, the picture of uncertainty.

"It wasn't the right time." The words proved harder to say than he'd expected, but as he heard them in his own voice, he understood them to be true. Though he didn't understand the wait, he trusted that God had been faithful in the unknown of the last four and a half years.

The fidgeting stopped. Her brown irises lifted.

In her expression, he saw confirmation. God had been faithful, and his wait for her to return his feelings was finally over.

He smirked. "What you shouldn't have done was make me promise to never ask again, because now my hands are tied."

Her jaw dropped, then a smile bloomed as she seemed to realize they were on the same page. All that was left was to figure out how to turn to the next one, advancing from best friends to more.

"I never made you promise. I just—" She swatted playfully at his shoulder, but he caught her hand.

Caught and held it. Despite the instant fist she formed, she didn't pull away.

Her smile sobered. She licked her lips. "... told you there would be consequences if you ever did."

"Remind me." He applied gentle pressure to the side of her fist with his thumb. A request, not a demand. "What are the consequences?"

Her fingers unclenched but didn't intertwine with his. "Besides the possible ones to our friendship and your career?"

"Besides those."

Her palm turned to meet his. She stared at the connection. "I can't actually think of any."

He'd been hoping one of the consequences might be a kiss, but his whole arm buzzed from the touch of her hand. More might short-circuit his heart. "I am willing to risk—"

"Oh!" Her fingers tightened around his. "Heartbreak. That could be a consequence."

He closed her hand between both of his. "I'm willing to risk all of it, including heartbreak. Are you?"

Her eyebrows formed worried lines.

"I promise to be careful with you. With us."

The lines on her forehead eased. The corners of her mouth remained downturned.

"We know each other," he said. "If it is a risk to try something new, it's an educated one. We already have things we like to do together. I always enjoy your company. About the only aspect of a relationship we've never explored is chemistry."

Her gaze zipped up to meet his.

He swallowed. If she turned him down after this next admission, the confession might make it harder for her to accept him back into the friend zone. But he'd assured her he was willing to take risks to make this work. This was his chance to make good on that promise. "There's never been a lack of chemistry on my side."

Her lips parted, but neither a frown nor a smile gave hints about why.

He resisted clearing his throat, but then the attraction he'd suppressed for years rumbled in his next words. "How about yours?"

She bit her bottom lip. "There is something I've been wondering that I've never considered about my other friends."

"What's that?"

Her lashes flicked as her gaze dropped to his mouth.

She'd been thinking about kissing him.

How long had *that* been going on?

"If I tell you," she breathed, "there's probably no going back."

Staring at his mouth like that, she'd see his smirk, but he couldn't help it. "You could show me instead."

She tilted her head, focus lifting as she narrowed a glare at him. "Then there'd *really* be no going back."

"I don't want to go back."

Her irises were layered with rich browns, coffee to mahogany—details he couldn't have noticed if this topic hadn't drawn them closer together than they'd been when they first sat. Decision settled in her features, and her lashes fanned closed. He watched her lean in until he could feel the warmth of her breath, then let his own eyes ease shut.

Since she'd joined him tonight, she'd been flighty and uncertain, so different from the Neenah he knew. If that had been the Neenah that kissed him, he would've had the first of the heartbreak he'd sworn to endure. He didn't want her to feel insecure with him or about their potential. He wanted her to feel safe. Protected. Confident enough in his loyalty to her that she could be her decisive, brave, direct self.

And judging by the press of her lips on his, she did. She untangled their hands, and her fingers found their way along his jaw then curled around the back of his neck, as if he needed any encouragement to come closer, stretch the moment, and taste the fulfillment of years of daydreams.

He was kissing Neenah. *He was kissing Neenah.*

He needed her closer. Without breaking the kiss, he drew her with him to standing and she rewarded him by melting against him.

He'd expected a kiss to change everything. He'd thought the past would fall away and leave them with something completely new. Instead, when they parted, he saw reminders of all their years of friendship. Pink flushed her cheeks as it did after a good workout. Her eyes glittered like when she beat him at something—initiating a kiss.

He'd even the score next time.

But there was new territory here too, unexplored and inviting. She dragged her fingers through his hair, her body still against his in a relaxed embrace the likes of which they'd never shared before.

They hadn't lost their friendship. They'd expanded it.

Yet what they'd discussed beforehand remained true. If this became a casualty of his dad's disapproval or of long distance, should she take a job elsewhere, there'd be no going back. They'd either overcome the difficulties or they'd each be on the market for a new best friend.

Chapter Eleven

At some point, Neenah needed to tell Kaylie about the change with Cody. But how, when the moment shimmered in her memory like a dream and not reality? She cracked an egg into the frying pan. To the soundtrack of its sizzling, she replayed the kiss once again.

She'd initiated the contact, but Cody took the lead pulling her to her feet and deepening the kiss. Their years of friendship had offered hints of what it might be like to be cradled to his chest, but never had she imagined the way his lips on hers, his arms holding her up, his heart beating so close to hers would overwhelm her senses. Even now, the heat of it made her step away from the stove and fan her face. As if the burner explained the heady rush.

So maybe the memory of the kiss was real—a little too much so, in fact.

Kaylie hunched over her phone, oblivious as she shoveled dripping cereal into her mouth. The school transfer had finally come through. Soon, they'd drive to her first day of classes, then Neenah would continue to Second Chances for a shift. Big announcements about Cody could wait.

The smell of hot bread turned her to check on her toast a second before the lever released and the bread popped up. She assembled her plate.

When she sat at the table, Kaylie pressed a button on her phone. Her attention fixed on Neenah. "You were out late."

A blush nipped at her cheeks. Again, the kiss sped through her mind in glorious detail, from the stomach-twisting anticipation to the exhilaration of being so thoroughly welcomed.

"How's Cody?" Kaylie's blue eyes danced.

"He's good." She bit into her toast because she wasn't sure how else to keep from grinning. Too bad she'd forgotten to add butter, and doing so now would advertise how flustered she was. She pushed a bite of egg onto the bread and ate the two together. Much better. "How are you feeling about starting school?"

Kaylie smirked as if she saw right through her. "I like the idea of having only a couple of days before Christmas break. That way, I can ease into it. Meet everybody, find out how far behind I am, and then spend the next week and a half catching up."

"You plan to spend your break studying?"

She shrugged. "Yeah. It's not like I haven't already had a big break, right?"

"You haven't been in school, but you've been busy."

"I've been in *limbo*." Her posture worsened like an inflatable lawn ornament with the air pump turned off. "Having extra time off school isn't as great as I always thought it'd be."

Neenah lowered her fork. "That's because the circumstances are terrible. Whether you wanted it or not, you needed time."

"You didn't?"

"What would I need time for?" She cut another bite of toast and egg.

"You lost something too."

"Yeah, but—"

Kaylie's chin dipped with a warning. "Mom used to say 'yeah, but' was another way of saying no."

"Fair enough. All I was going to say is that my situation is different from yours."

"Except we both hate sitting around being sad, and that's why you got a job so quick, even though you don't like it, and why you're risking your life on the neighborhood watch."

"I'm not risking my life, honey." She'd never been the type to use terms of endearment before, but with Kaylie, they slipped out. "It's very safe. And that's why I got the job I did —to minimize risk." At Kaylie's request. Although the mention of risk brought back Cody's solemn declaration that he'd risk heartbreak and more to be with her.

"You didn't have to take the first safe job that came along. You could've kept looking until you found something you at least kind of liked. But you didn't because you were in a hurry to be busy again."

Neenah swallowed hard. Was that true? And did it apply to the recent developments with Cody? Was she just trying to stay busy? To fill a void?

Kaylie continued. "That's what I want too—to get out of the house more. Days are way too long when all you get to do is sit around and think all the time."

Neenah nudged her plate away. "I hope you haven't felt like you've had nothing to do this whole time. We've been running, attending town events, decorating ..." She left off therapy, chores, and the rhythms of everyday life. "Is there something we've been missing?"

"Just school." She tilted her phone toward Neenah to display the time. "Speaking of, it's time to go."

"Okay. Get your things. I'll be ready in a minute." Her appetite hadn't returned, but she choked down the last of her breakfast to avoid being ravenous by lunchtime. After dropping Kaylie off, she continued to Second Chances.

From the parking lot, she squinted at the building. Her retirement hadn't been a surprise. She'd had time to look for work beforehand, but she'd figured after losing the only job she'd ever wanted, she would need time to get her head around the loss and to find an alternative that felt just as tailor-made for her as police work. She'd wanted to give herself that gift—time off.

In the end, she'd been as grateful for it as Kaylie. Unlike Kaylie, however, no obstacle course of paperwork had slowed her down from moving on to the next thing in a desperate search for a new purpose in life. And so, from Kaylie to this job to Cody, she'd careened into a whole new life, making who knew how many mistakes along the way.

* * *

Cody parked at the back of the police station parking lot. This ought to be the best day of his life. His favorite and best dream had come true. But reporting to work under his father's command was like chugging orange juice right after brushing his teeth. Extraordinarily bitter.

He needed to confront his dad about the threats he'd made to Neenah regarding their careers. About meddling in their lives well beyond their jobs at the station. However, as he approached the building, a logo-emblazoned news van squatted by the main entrance. A clean-cut reporter with a microphone stood beside Burt Quince in front of the cameraman. Chief Adams flanked his temporary detective.

Any confrontation would have to wait.

To get inside, Cody would have to cut directly behind them, almost as close to the camera as his father was. He clenched his jaw and hung back. These segments usually lasted no more than a minute or two.

The reporter's voice carried in the quiet morning. "Given the thief has been stealing Christmas decorations, do you think it's fair to say the perpetrator is against the holiday?"

Leaving coal seemed like a way of participating in a Christmas tradition, rather than fighting against it. Cody would give a quick *no* to the question.

That wasn't Quince's style, though. Not when tempted by the lure of fame—as limited and short-lived as it was sure to be. "Recovering some of the items by a recreational trail suggests the individual didn't intend to keep the items for him or herself. The motive could be a dislike for the holiday, or perhaps certain decorations became problematic for this individual. Maybe a neighbor's lights were keeping this person up at night."

Cody turned his scoff into clearing his throat. His dad cut him a glare. The other two didn't glance his way.

The reporter shared Cody's objection, however, because he said, "Surely, that doesn't explain so many different neighborhoods being hit."

"This is true." Burt tugged on his belt. "We haven't been able to find a link between victims of this crime, but we continue to investigate. Once we find a connection, a new motive may come to light."

Sounded like a good place to end the interview.

But the reporter wasn't finished. "Any thoughts on the reason for the yeti costume?"

Because it's a prank. The yeti's loving the attention even more than Quince.

"It's as good of a disguise as any." Quince smiled as if he wasn't yet another cop the yeti had managed to elude.

Chief retained a serious expression as he nodded his agreement. If he regretted transferring the investigation, he showed no signs of it. When was the last time his dad had backed him up the way he was supporting Burt Quince?

"Is such a costume traceable?" the reporter asked.

With no end to the interview in sight, Cody dipped his head and cut behind the group to reach the doors.

"No stores carry one locally, but in the internet age, anyone could've had one delivered to their doorstep, no one the wiser." At least the answer rang true instead of giving Cody reason to roll his eyes while in the background.

He stepped into the station, and the door cut off the rest of the interview. He powered up his computer to complete some paperwork. He hadn't gotten far when Chief and Quince entered.

"Good job." Chief patted Quince's shoulder. "Not everyone stays collected in interviews."

Quince nodded an acknowledgement, then stepped away.

Good job?

Cody couldn't remember the last time his father had called his work good. He stood and stepped around his desk, on path to follow his father into his office for a long overdue conversation.

"Adams." As Chief issued the gruff summons, he turned. His eyebrows shot up in surprise that Cody was already in pursuit.

About time Cody got the upper hand.

It was short-lived as his dad took up station behind his desk. Instead of sinking into the chair, the man remained standing and leafed through paperwork. Apparently, Cody wasn't even worthy of eye contact. "You missed the yeti last night."

No one had caught the yeti yet, but the one his father called to account? His son, who wasn't even on the case. Meanwhile, Quince had done a good job.

Chief studied one of the papers. "You weren't alone."

"No, I wasn't."

"You were with Neenah Casper."

"I had an interesting talk with her. She says you told her you wanted me to be chief someday."

His father's head shifted, a minute sign of surprise. "At one point, I did hope for that."

"What changed?"

"You don't want to hear it." Still foregoing eye contact, Chief laid down the paper and sat. His back remained straight, but he adjusted his seat as if he couldn't find the right distance from his desk.

"What I heard from her is that my advancement—and hers—depended on us not dating. We didn't, yet aside from the fact that I earned a master's degree, I'm no closer to a promotion than I was four and a half years ago. Same for Neenah, up until her retirement. So, I'll ask again. What changed?"

"You didn't want it." He enunciated, the sounds as sharp as a collection of knives.

"Are you kidding me?"

Finally, his father lifted his eyes in a flare of challenge. "When I brought you in and offered the chance you're squandering now, you explained yourself why you didn't pursue detective sooner. You didn't want it. And though I didn't hear the words from your mouth before then, I knew. You're my son. I know you better than you think."

Cody clenched his jaw and turned his face, absorbing the blow. "Because I was willing to let a friend get ahead first, you assumed I didn't want it? Graham needed a better way to support his family."

"Everyone has good reasons for wanting a promotion. Who—besides my son—doesn't want better pay and hours? More autonomy? You stand back for one person, and where does it end?"

"The very next time a spot opened up. I put my name in."

His father's lips thinned, and his gaze slipped away to a corner.

The truth hit him like a bullet. "You advised against promoting me then."

His father swatted a hand through the air in dismissal. "Finally, you have the chance to prove you want the promotion, and you haven't closed a case. Not only that, but you divided your focus with a woman when you could've caught a break on the decoration thefts. It's self-sabotage. I have no reason to believe that behavior would cease if you got what you supposedly wanted."

"My cases have been harder than Quince's—and that's why he's still struggling with the decoration thefts. As for Neenah, she's not a random woman. She's the only reason I was out looking for the yeti to begin with. We make a good team, and for some reason that threatens you? Scares you? Because I can't imagine why else you'd stand in our way."

"That's what this is about. You've got yourself convinced you belong together and I kept you apart? But if that fantasy were true, my little talk with her wouldn't have stood between you. You're indifferent to her, and I have to believe she is to you."

She'd been traumatized by childhood experiences, not indifferent.

And Cody had given up pursuing her because it was the only way to stay in her circle. He pulled his shoulders back. Shook his head. "Do you even know the meaning of sacrifice?"

"There's a difference between sacrifice and martyrdom. Adams men fight for what they want, and you're a doormat."

"Or maybe I'm fighting for different things."

Chief snorted and shook his head.

How had Cody never seen before the chasm between his

own values and his father's? "If that's how you see me, give the promotion to Quince."

Maybe the statement was a test. One last attempt to make his father see the harm in his fault finding and change course.

But before Chief could respond, an officer knocked and stuck her head in. "Another burglary. This time, someone got hurt."

Chapter Twelve

An older man sat on the curb, shoulders slouched under his winter jacket. His hands rested on the knees of his sweatpants, and he stared blankly toward his all-black orthopedic sneakers. Cody parked behind the other squad cars as Jake, a paramedic he had worked with before, checked the man over. A white-haired woman perched next to the patient. The couple looked familiar, but from where?

Not church. Somewhere else.

Another woman hovered on the sidewalk and wrung her hands, so focused on the patient she didn't notice Cody approach. This lady, he knew. Despite being well past retirement age, Mrs. Rasinski worked mornings at her son and daughter-in-law's donut shop.

Scenes like this always filled Cody with a sense of purpose while waiting for a detective position to open up. Patrol officers had the honor and responsibility of assisting people on some of the worst days of their lives. Whether or not detective was in his future, he still believed in providing aid and reassurance, serving the community, and pursuing justice.

He got out his notepad. "Did you call?"

Mrs. Rasinski's cornflower-blue eyes flicked to him, then back to the patient. She exhaled a shaky breath. "It was awful. We saw a man in a mask loading things from a three-tier utility cart into a truck. Ernie shouted for him to stop, but he loaded the last item before Ernie got there."

"Got there?" Cody's pen stopped mid-word.

"He pushed Ernie down, threw the cart in the bed, and careened out of here. He almost took out me and Bev." She waved toward the other woman. "She's married to Ernie, by the way. Bev and Ernie Schilling." She glanced at his abandoned notes.

He scribbled the names down. "You approached?"

"Ernie did—we stayed on the sidewalk. Bev tried to stop him from going, but he said, 'Not on my watch,' and off he went."

The word 'watch' filled in the blank. He'd noticed the man—one of the few males at the neighborhood watch meeting. Ernie Schilling had signed up for a daily patrol. This wasn't his scheduled early-morning shift, though.

"What were you doing when you saw the man?"

"Walking and keeping an eye on things. Ernie and Bev are part of the neighborhood watch, and that sounded exciting, so why not tag along? But then things went so poorly. You're going to catch the man, right? I heard this isn't his first crime."

It *was* his first with injuries. He needed to talk to Neenah about the neighborhood watch. And Clara should post a warning so no citizens approached if they saw a crime in progress. If only it hadn't come to this. Was his father onto something? Could he have done more to wrap up this investigation sooner?

"Did you get a license plate?"

"Oh." The flush drained from her cheeks. "Everything happened so fast."

Frustration crackled in his chest, but in the heat of the moment, plenty of witnesses missed details. They'd work with what she got. "Can you describe the man and his truck?"

"Oh, yes. About this tall." She held her hand over her head, indicating a few inches shorter than Cody. "Black ski mask. Black jacket. Not heavy, but not skinny, either. Medium?"

"And the truck?"

She waved a pointed finger as though to emphasize her crowning observation. "A white pickup."

At least the description matched what he'd learned at other scenes, increasing the odds that all the burglaries traced back to one perpetrator. That was something.

Meanwhile, other officers arrived, and the paramedics loaded Ernie onto a gurney. Cody took his leave from Mrs. Rasinski and approached the Schillings.

Jake stepped away from the gurney for an aside. "We suspect a broken wrist, and he hit his head. He can talk to you, but keep it brief."

"Will do." Cody approached the rolling stretcher.

Ernie's wrist lay propped across his torso, covered in ice packs. He rested his head against the gurney and a second cold compress. His pallor and slumped posture added a good fifteen years—and the man hadn't been young to start with.

"Mr. Schilling?"

Watery eyes lifted to Cody with all the energy of a sloth. Seeing someone capable reduced to a specter with the flashing lights around them reminded him of last winter. Of Neenah's injury. Of how close this elderly trio came to tragedy.

This case should've been solved by now. As the lead on the case, Cody, more than anyone else, was responsible for stopping him. Cody. Not Neenah and her neighborhood watch. They needed to back off before anyone else stepped into harm's way.

He mustered a sympathetic smile for Mr. Schilling. "Can you tell me what happened?"

The man grew more animated as he retold events that lined up with Mrs. Rasinski's statement. "If you catch the guy, I swear I'll be able to pick him out of a lineup by his ... by his ..." Ernie pointed a finger toward his own face and wiggled it back and forth across the bridge of his nose.

If the suspect had an wiggly scar over the bridge of his nose, identification would get a lot easier.

"... brown eyes," Mr. Schilling finished.

The most common eye color in the world. Of course.

While it didn't rule out too many others, Gary Jones had pale green irises. If he was involved, he had an accomplice.

Cody wrapped up the interview. As the ambulance rolled away to deliver Mr. Schilling to the hospital for follow-up, he connected with Justin, who'd arrived before him.

The other officer consulted his notes as they made their way toward the house. "The window in the back door was broken, door left open. The first-floor TVs were taken. He tossed the closets like he was looking for something."

They entered the living room, where Garrett met them. "We called the homeowner. He's on his way." He motioned over his shoulder with his pen. "He told us there should be a laptop there. Other than that, we won't know what else is missing until he gets here."

"And here I am."

Cody turned to find a windblown man. Though they'd never interacted much, the Redemption Ridge native had been a few years ahead of Cody in school. "Kent Greely."

The man nodded. "I can't believe this happened. And right before Christmas too. I hope he didn't find the gifts we hid away."

"Gifts?" Cody asked.

"Yeah. My wife and I put them on an upper shelf in the garage in hopes the kids wouldn't come across them."

"Were these gifts electronics?"

"Some of them—a virtual gaming system and some headphones."

"When and where did you purchase them?"

"Tech City. My wife picked them up a few weeks ago. Not Black Friday. I remember she was happy they were on sale a few days before so she didn't have to fight huge crowds."

"Okay. We'd better start there. Can you show us?"

Kent led them across the back patio and unlocked the detached garage. They crossed the oil-spotted concrete to a utility shelf.

Kent peered up through the plastic grate that served as the top shelf. "Ha!" Grinning, he stepped back and pointed. "He didn't get them."

Cody, too, felt a flare of satisfaction. A homeowner had finally won. In part. "Can you walk us through the rest of the house and let us know what he *did* take?"

Kent's grin faded, and they returned to the house. By the time he saw his belongings strewn across the floor and all the blanks where their TVs, game systems, and laptops should've been, his mouth settled into a grim line. The family had a lot of electronics to lose, and little set aside in the garage.

It was up to Cody to stop this loss of property, the violation of people's homes, and, most importantly, the injuries.

* * *

Neenah parted the hangers and snugged a skirt onto the rack. At least returning items discarded in the fitting rooms allowed her mind to focus on other tasks. Namely, on praying about all her recent choices. Had she been following the Lord's lead, or hurrying to fill a void? And how would she know the difference?

"Are you okay?" Piper's voice came from behind her.

She took a sweater off the cart and straightened it on the hanger. "Yes, just a lot on my mind."

"There must be. You're in the dress pants section."

Neenah's hands dropped, and the sweater bumped against her leg. All down the rack, the shoulders of shirts protruded from between the narrower pant hangers.

Piper giggled, stepped down to the opposite end, and withdrew the first few shirts. "What are you so absorbed thinking about?"

Neenah worked backward to meet her. "How do you know what God wants you to choose when you face a decision?"

Piper shot her a half-grimace, half-smile. "Nothing big on your mind, then."

Neenah laughed despite herself. "It's just hard to know sometimes when there's not a clear moral right and wrong."

"I get that." Piper returned a shimmery blouse to the cart. "If it's not a question of sin, maybe God has an adventure planned for you either way."

"Like I can't choose wrong?"

"As long as you're choosing God."

That was a freeing way to look at it ... but could she say she'd been choosing God when she rushed into a job and fell into a romance? Or had she been choosing the closest options that looked like they might restore purpose to her days?

"What decision has you so tied up?" As Piper asked, a bell jingled. Someone had entered through the back door, but the customer hadn't made it down the hall and into sight yet. "If you don't mind my asking, that is."

A tricky question to answer, considering work at Second

Chances was one of her hang-ups. And if she mentioned Cody, the reaction was sure to be big.

A dark-blue shape materialized where the back hall emptied into the store—Cody, in uniform and looking broad and strong and official. Her stomach flipped. She'd kissed that man last night. What was left to debate?

He spotted her. His expression, stony as a mountain, didn't lighten up. Her waffling confidence tipped the other way again. Something was wrong. What if he was having second thoughts too?

Desperation thrummed in her chest. Suddenly, she knew what she wanted—Cody. His support had been carrying her for years. She couldn't do without him.

A knowing hum ripped Neenah's focus to Piper. Her boss covered her mouth, but her eyes danced. If Piper could tell something had changed just by looking at them, she also ought to recognize the trouble in Cody's expression.

He headed their way and dipped his head in greeting. "Ladies."

Had his voice always sounded gravelly, or were all her observations about him filtered through hormones now?

"I'll be in the office if you need me." Piper fled, whisper-singing, "But I doubt you will."

Cody didn't spare her a glance. His focus was too intent on Neenah. "Some of your neighborhood watchers had a run-in with the burglar."

"Oh, no." And he'd come to tell her in person. With that expression. The altercation must've been serious. "Who? What happened?"

"The older gentleman who signed up for early-morning shifts. Ernie Schilling. He was out for a walk with two lady friends and came across the burglar loading up at the Greely household. Mr. Schilling tried to stop him and got pushed over for his trouble. Concussion and a broken wrist."

At the meeting, Ernie's voice had been gruff as he'd asserted the importance of protecting the neighborhood. Even the way he'd carried himself, chest puffed up and elbows back, had spoken of a commitment to do what needed doing to ensure the safety of the community. Perhaps she should've known he'd break protocol and approach a criminal, but it wasn't like she could control him. Perhaps even his wife couldn't. "*Two* lady friends?"

"His wife and Mrs. Rasinski, who both thankfully stayed out of harm's way."

"Good. Any new leads?"

Cody narrowed his eyes as if she'd asked the wrong question. "Nothing helpful, except that the Greelys also shopped at Tech City recently."

"It's getting pretty brazen for them to hit only people who shop there."

"Most people in town do, and we don't have anything on any of the employees." He glanced out the windows and refocused on her. "A fact I'll let them know today, so that if it is one of them, they'll stay brave enough for one last job."

"You have a plan?"

"Which is why I need you to call off the neighborhood watch. I can't have our operation interrupted."

Pressure built in her lungs, but shouting demands that he trust her with the particulars wouldn't be any more effective than begging Chief to allow her back onto the force. "I imagine Ernie learned his lesson. With a concussion and a broken bone, he'll need to rest up anyway."

Cody shook his head, the line between his eyebrows deepening. "The group was one thing before either of the ongoing sprees involved violence. Since that changed, we need to let the authorities handle it."

"We?" She scanned his uniform again. Maybe it wasn't so attractive after all. She rested a fist on her cocked hip. "You can't group yourself with me and the watch if you're also among these authorities you want me to cower behind."

"It's not cowering, Neenah." He shifted closer, frustration harsh in his voice. "It's admitting what's working and what isn't. The yeti struck right under our noses, and we didn't learn a thing. And who's to say he won't get violent, too, if he's cornered? Mr. Schilling is lucky his injuries weren't worse—at his age, they're bad enough."

"I don't want anything to happen to anyone, but Ernie won't be going out again. I'm sure the others will heed the warning."

Cody crossed his arms over his chest. "There's no benefit to continuing. Only risk."

"Some risks are worth it. Remember?" Her traitorous eyes dipped to his lips, only to find them pressed into a stern line. She stepped closer, lifted a hand, hesitated. Would he allow her touch or move away?

He only watched.

She trailed her fingertips from his shoulder to his chest but felt little besides the starchy fabric of his shirt, the firm contours of the armored vest underneath, and a badge she didn't get to wear anymore. She dropped her hand. "I'm not calling off the watch. Two situations that didn't go our way doesn't mean they'll all end the same. Maybe both thieves will be spooked by how close they came to being caught. Maybe they'll stop *because* of the watch."

"Or maybe they'll rise to the challenge and become even more dangerous."

She matched his crossed arms by banding her own over her body. "What's this plan of yours? The one to catch the burglar?"

"We have someone making a purchase from Tech City that matches the MO. We're going to put an electronic tracker in the boxes and wait."

At least he'd shared. She could see a few potential problems, though. "This is a small town. If a local is behind the burglaries, he or she probably knows who the cops are and won't try to rob one of them."

"We're sending someone else."

"A citizen."

"Yes."

"So it's okay when you involve civilians, but not when they're part of the neighborhood watch."

"The couple is going to stay with friends until the New Year or we catch the guy, whichever comes first. They'll be out of harm's way."

That meant that he'd given her only the briefest version of the plan. Most likely, the setup involved several steps he hadn't revealed. If he expected blind trust from her, she deserved the same. "I'll make sure my watchers keep more distance, but I'm not calling it off."

"You don't have the resources the police department has. I'm not going to have a civilian bumping into a police operation. And you shouldn't want your people wandering into trouble."

"Fine. I'll tell them to stand down, but I'm still patrolling. I might not be official anymore, but I can help the town too."

"Neenah ..." Pity softened the warning in his tone. "Don't."

Her eyes burned and her throat felt swollen, but she refused to give in to the impulse to cry. "Don't what?"

"You're even more likely than Ernie Schilling to take things into your own hands. Stay home with Kaylie."

That was all she was good for in his eyes? Babysitting? Only she couldn't ask, because then the tears would come. All these years, she'd thought he respected her as an equal.

"You had to retire for a reason," he continued in his unreasonably soft tone. If he was going to rip up their relationship, he could at least raise his voice. "Chasing down criminals would be hard on your knees, not to mention the danger of going it alone."

Anger lent her the fortitude to speak. "I'm not some—some antique vase you can bubble wrap and stick on a shelf. I don't know what you think that kiss meant, but it wasn't a license to control me." Her nose burned and her throat ached, but at least her eyes remained dry.

Tension tightened his jaw and the skin around his eyes. "I don't know what *you* think the kiss meant, but I'm not—and have never been—a doormat. I'm trying to do a job here. You need to let me."

"A doormat? Where is that coming from?"

"You've called all the shots in our friendship about when we could be more, and that's fine. I waited for you. I supported your decisions. And I was happy to do it. But this one thing." He jabbed a pointed finger at the floor as if the stakeout was the foundation he stood on. "Is it really too much to ask? Call off the watch until we catch these clowns. You can pick it up again after."

"You don't mind me doing a neighborhood watch when there's nothing to report. You want me to wait until I'm useless. Because I'm not already useless enough with my bionic knees."

"Neenah, please." Pain etched his features. "You know your worth better than that, and you know me better than that. I'm asking for one thing."

"You must not know me as well as you think, because my purpose is one thing I can't give up. Not even for you." She grabbed the cart of clothing and shoved it down the aisle away from him, even though that meant taking the long way around the displays to the rack where the shirts were actually supposed to hang.

By the time she circled around, he was gone.

Chapter Thirteen

Neenah was called to serve her community. After her fight with Cody, she went back to praying. Hard. Trying to discern God's will for her messed-up life. The ache over the argument wouldn't ease, but she also couldn't give up the one project that contributed toward her life's purpose as she'd always known it.

She had to believe that Cody would come around, especially once he heard her dutifully call in any trouble instead of chasing it down herself.

So, at nine, she parked her truck on Main Street and watched from the safety of the driver's seat. All the garlands and lights offered the yeti the opportunity for the biggest Christmas decoration caper yet. Surely, he couldn't resist forever.

She sipped from the travel mug of hot cocoa Kaylie had poured for her before she headed out. Though she doubted the yeti would de-escalate to as small of a target as her measly wreath and strings of lights, she kept her phone on the dash mount, ready to alert her to any calls from Kaylie or blips on the security cameras. Barring those circumstances, for the next hour, it was just her, her truck, and Main Street.

Then Cody's shift with the watch would start. Did he plan to follow through? His choice would be telling for their relationship, but that was as out of her control as Ernie's decisions.

Some of the businesses had apartments above them, and a restaurant or two still served customers. Strings of lights, mostly white, decorated storefronts, and garlands and bows graced the old-fashioned streetlamps. Below-freezing weather dropped the occasional snowflake on the few pedestrians who hurried from one building to another or to parked cars.

No one, not even the people she eyed in the passing vehicles, wore a furry costume or paused to mess with the décor. Flakes swirled onto her windshield, and her breath fogged the air. She took another sip of cocoa. Forty-three minutes to go.

Her phone lit up, but instead of signaling an emergency, the notification informed her Kaylie had sent a cat reel. She chuckled to herself. Opening her home to the sweet teenager was the one recent decision she didn't doubt.

Thanking God for the light the girl brought to her life, Neenah watched the reel. The cat fell into and vaulted out of a bathtub. The street stayed quiet. She replied with a GIF before returning the phone to its mount.

Thirty-nine minutes.

Headlights advanced slowly down Main. A white truck, like the home burglar drove. He'd always struck during the day, but he could be casing some place. Or perhaps the driver was drunk or lost. If she were a cop, she'd fall in line behind him.

Without that option at her disposal, she leaned into the shadows of her cab where the driver wouldn't notice her. He peered one way, then the other. Looking for something, but what?

She cataloged what details she could about the driver—short hair, a thick neck, and bulky shoulders. Not the yeti—at least, not in costume. Through the static of increasing snowfall, she read his license plate.

Once he'd passed, she grabbed her phone and pulled up her message thread with Cody. Her thumbs hovered without typing.

He didn't approve of this, so he wouldn't want a tip from her. And yet, she'd stayed in her vehicle. And she was more than halfway through the hour she'd planned to stake out Main Street. Then, she'd go home and, hopefully, Cody would pick up where she left off with the watch, and they would talk tomorrow. Resolve their differences.

She chewed her lip. Usually, he was the first to reach out after a disagreement, and part of her was always happy to see or hear from him. To know that whatever had gone wrong, they'd come back together, work it out, move forward as friends.

Or, now, more than friends.

There was no reason she couldn't be the one to break the silence this time. Well, no reason besides her pride. Oh, and the fact that she'd disobeyed his order to stop the neighborhood watch.

Maybe the truck was nothing.

Or maybe it was something, and the Lord had allowed her to see the suspicious behavior so she could act on it.

NEENAH

Is your stakeout on Main?

CODY

No. Why?

Such a quick, short answer might indicate he was still

angry. He was about to be more so, probably, when she showed her hand, but she'd come this far.

NEENAH

White truck just rolled by slowly, looking for something. Male driver.

She ended with the license plate and sent it off.

CODY

He stop?

NEENAH

No. Gone.

CODY

Thanks. I'll run the plate.

Nine minutes passed.

CODY

No one related to the burglary case, but I'll keep a note of it.

So her big tip was for nothing. She ought to just be grateful that her decision to go ahead with a neighborhood watch shift hadn't reignited their argument.

Twenty-one minutes to go.

Lord, is he the right one for me? How about the neighborhood watch? Was I right to fight for it?

She squinted into the snow. It brightened the scene but obscured the view. Maybe God did want her with Cody so someone could talk her out of activities like the neighborhood watch. After all, He had allowed her to lose her job with the police. Maybe these next—she checked the time again—eleven minutes ought to be the very last patrol of her life.

Her breath stuttered in and out, the future considerably darker than the light-sprinkled street before her. Not that she could see it very well with snow on her windshield. She put the truck in accessory mode and swiped the wipers. Moments afterward, one of the storefronts went dark.

Her eyes fixed on the area. The lights strung from the awning could've been on a timer. No one walked near there, unless there was something she couldn't see because of the snow and parked vehicles.

Her hand found her seat buckle to investigate on foot, but Cody's favorite warning rang in her mind. She huffed and turned the key instead. The engine rumbled like an avalanche on the quiet street.

The concessions she made for love.

Her eyes went wide, and she froze, but now was not the time to unpack why that word had slipped into her thoughts.

She pulled into the lane and accelerated as slowly as she dared.

No yeti spooled up lights in the shadows—as far as she could see over the vehicles—but a dark figure rounded the corner of the building and disappeared into the adjacent alleyway.

She swerved into the nearest open spot and twisted in her seat. She knew the alley. The brick-paved path boasted flowers in summer, park benches that hearty residents used even in winter, and small trees some committee or other decorated for Christmas. Come to think of it, the lights on the branches hadn't been illuminated when she'd passed.

She dialed the station. "I think the Christmas decoration thief might be in the alley of the 200 block of Main Street, taking lights off the trees." If only she could see down the alley from where she'd parked.

The operator asked a couple of questions and promised to dispatch a unit.

Neenah disconnected and drummed her fingers against her phone. A minute ticked by.

This was taking entirely too long.

The yeti wasn't dangerous, and he wouldn't be cornered in that alley. It led to a parking lot behind the businesses with exits on either side. Anyway, she wouldn't risk damaging her knees to sprint after a guy in a yeti costume, meaning he could outpace her and disappear. But perhaps if she got close enough first, she could provide the police with a new lead— like a license plate number.

Still no headlights—and definitely no reds and blues— advanced toward her location.

She hopped out, eased her door shut, and jogged to the storefront. Lights still hung from the bars supporting the awning overhead, so those hadn't been stolen. She peeked around the corner.

No one in sight, but the yeti might have ducked behind the trash can or one of the evergreen bushes. Surely, he couldn't have untangled several trees' worth of lights already and fled. She waited, peering around the corner in case he hadn't left the area and would get back to work.

What now, God?

Like an answer to prayer, an engine chugged to life and light flashed from the parking lot beyond. He was getting away —and that was fine. She only needed the plate number. She jogged to the lot, stepped off the curb, and looked toward the noise. Headlights careened toward her.

She leaped for the safety of the curb, but her foot slipped. Pain hit like lightning—hot, fast, and followed by darkness.

* * *

What a long, horrible day. To think, less than twenty-four hours ago, Cody and Neenah had shared their first kiss after his neighborhood watch shift. Now, as ten o'clock neared, he debated heading out on the informal patrol.

He'd asked her to call it off but not out of concern for his own safety. The problem was, patrolling the town for an hour would take him away from his desk, where he could keep a close eye on the app paired with the GPS transmitter he'd placed in the bait from Tech City. He and the others involved in the stakeout had done everything they could to encourage the burglar, whoever it was, to hit tonight.

"He got under your skin again, didn't he?"

Cody lifted a hand from the keyboard and rested his elbow on the desktop.

Graham swung a neighboring desk chair around, sat at the edge of Cody's workspace, and used the surface as an armrest. He'd pulled a jacket over a hooded sweatshirt, and his curly hair frizzed to twice the volume as usual.

"Shouldn't you be home with your family?"

He tried—in vain—to flatten his hair, as if he knew which part of his appearance had prompted the question. "Who do you think sent me?"

Oh. Piper had seen him at Second Chances. Even if Neenah hadn't shared the details of their disagreement, it wouldn't take a professional investigator to conclude their conversation hadn't gone well. "How much did she tell you?"

"Where to start ..." Graham settled back as if to read fairy-tales to his kids. "Neenah didn't say much, but Piper says she'd bet her store you two kissed, because, to quote the witness, the air between you was 'charged' as soon as you walked in the store. But you argued and it didn't end well. I'm thinking if you finally got somewhere with Neenah, there's no way you'd mess it up so soon, unless maybe that conversation I saw you have with your dad earlier threw you off."

"Maybe it did." After all, he had felt the need to tell Neenah he wasn't a doormat. As if making a claim was the same as proving his mettle. "But I don't know if I can blame him for being right."

"About what?"

He bumped his fist against the desktop. Couldn't see a way out of direct honesty, even if the truth reflected badly on him. "You think I'm sabotaging myself? I knew Neenah wouldn't give up the watch, but I told her to anyway. And I told Chief to give the promotion to Quince."

Graham sat forward and shot a look around. "Careful, he's around here somewhere."

Cody motioned to the desk across the room where Quince pecked away at his keyboard. He claimed to be catching up on paperwork. More likely, he wanted to be nearby if the yeti was spotted or to hear if the home burglar GPS tag moved. Not that Cody would let Quince beat him to an arrest, even if he had surrendered the promotion.

Graham settled back again. "If you did those things, you had reasons."

Spoken like a true, blindly trusting friend.

"One of them being I've been waiting so long, I don't know what to do with opportunities anymore."

"No." Graham laughed. "Not that."

The dismissiveness would annoy him, except that the confidence had to come from somewhere. "Then what's your theory?"

"Your dad's not a bad boss for everybody else, but he seems determined to be unhappy with you, no matter what you do." Graham frowned toward Chief's office. "It makes sense to tell him you're done jumping through his hoops. If he does give Quince the job over you, he'll pay for it in the long run, and even he knows it."

"Maybe. But I shouldn't have taken my frustrations with him out on Neenah. It just ... felt ..." He shifted in his seat. He'd gone into the store angry, and when he'd left, he'd been the same. But on the way out, his life had felt a little more familiar than it had before things with Neenah fell apart.

He *had* sabotaged their relationship.

He'd claimed to be willing to risk anything to be with her, including heartbreak. Since he'd been living with the pain of unrequited feelings for her for years, that hadn't been much of a risk, had it? Heartbreak had been his holding pattern.

The joy of being together, however, had been completely new. Enjoying anything as much as he enjoyed the change between him and Neenah felt risky. Intolerably risky, considering the fight he'd picked.

What a fool. "I messed up."

Graham laughed ruefully and patted the edge of the desk. "My job here is done."

Cody picked up his phone. But what should he text her? Or should he call?

"Hey, Quince." The overnight receptionist stood at the entrance to the bull pen. "Yeti sighting downtown."

Burt hurried out.

Graham stood too. "If you and Neenah are moving ahead with a relationship, go easy on yourselves. Even good change is uncomfortable at first. Remember how much trouble Piper and I had finding a bedroom color we could both live with?"

About a month after the wedding, Graham and Piper sent their best friends—Cody and Lucy—to pick paint for them since they couldn't come to an agreement. "I don't blame you for objecting to purple."

"Yeah, I don't know how they labeled that shade gray." Graham covered a yawn. "Anyway. Growing pains are natural, and you have friends to support you."

He dipped his chin. "Thanks."

With a wave, Graham headed out.

Cody pulled up his text thread with Neenah and stewed over what to say. But then the display flashed Kaylie's name and a picture she'd taken of herself with his phone during the cookie decorating competition.

He swiped to answer. "Kaylie?"

"Neenah went out for the neighborhood watch and now she's not answering, but the yeti's here."

He eyed the exit. Quince was likely already rolling up on the scene of the other yeti sighting. If Neenah reported the first one, she might be catching Quince up on what she'd seen. That interaction could keep her from answering Kaylie's call. But the yeti couldn't be both downtown and at Neenah's, on the outskirts of Redemption Ridge.

Cody glanced at his computer screen. The GPS tracker hadn't budged. He moved toward the door. "What do you see?"

"A yeti. Well, a guy in a big fuzzy costume. He's on our front porch." She gasped. "Oh no."

"What?" Cody pushed through the exit and broke into a jog. Fresh snow blanketed everything.

Kaylie's voice came in a whispered hiss. "I think he saw me."

He sprinted. "I'm on my way." This time of night, with the roads quiet and lights flashing, he could get out to Neenah's in about five minutes. But as he rounded his squad car, his foot slipped. His shoe jammed into the tire of a neighboring vehicle, stopping his slide before he fell. With slick conditions, the drive would take a few extra minutes.

He got behind the wheel. As he pulled out of the lot, he radioed dispatch, then switched the phone to speaker. "What's he doing now?"

"I don't know. You want me to look again?"

"No." He sped through town.

Quince radioed about an injured pedestrian at the scene of the supposed yeti sighting. Maybe they had this backward— whoever called in the first yeti sighting had actually come across the home burglar with his proven capacity for injuries, so Quince was on his tail while Cody chased the yeti. At this point, they'd both just have to work the scenes they'd been called to.

"Is the door locked?" Cody asked.

"Um, I don't know." Scuffling sounds followed.

"Stay out of sight."

"I am. I'm crawling. I don't hear him anymore. I just— that doesn't necessarily mean he left, does it?" She sniffled. "Neenah said our lights weren't fancy enough and he'd leave us alone."

"She couldn't have known." A stop sign forced Cody to slow, in case traffic didn't see his lights in time to give him the right-of-way. No cars. He sped on.

"It's locked." Kaylie shuddered.

For feeling emotional, she seemed to be keeping it together. Could it be that having tasks was helping? "Go check the side door too."

He passed out of a residential area onto a straight, sparsely populated road that allowed him to accelerate. Deer collisions occurred on this stretch, and he prayed he wouldn't add to the statistic. "You doing all right, Kaylie?"

"Yeah. It's locked too. Are you almost here?"

"Two minutes."

"Okay. Okay." She blew out a deep breath. "Maybe if I look out my bedroom window, I can see what kind of car he drives. If he's still here."

"Don't risk it."

"He won't see me from here. I was in the living room before, and he was right on the porch. My bedroom isn't by any of our Christmas lights, and it has curtains. I can just peek out a little bit."

Cody turned onto Neenah's road, and the back end of the vehicle swung, tires skiing over the snow. As if she were in the car with him, Kaylie screamed.

A quick correction straightened him out in his lane. "Kaylie?"

"He was looking in my window! He was right there!"

"Lock yourself in the bathroom." He squinted into the darkness, but there weren't streetlights out here, and between darkness and snow, he couldn't make out any cars parked half a mile away, by Neenah's house. "Hang up and call 911."

"But you're coming, right?"

"Almost there. That's why I can't stay on the phone. They'll keep me updated."

"Okay." She disconnected.

The radio filled the silence. "Patrol two, transmitter at 36 Franklin has been activated."

His case, assigned to someone else.

The sting barely registered before Quince's voice came over the radio. "Attach me to the burglary. The incident on Main is not related to the yeti."

Frustration simmered. Cody couldn't change course when Kaylie needed him. He also couldn't object to Quince joining up with those responding to the burglar. That situation was more likely to require the manpower. Still. This had to be just the opportunity Quince had been waiting for.

He neared Neenah's house and spotted the first anomaly. The houses stood away from the road, yet someone had parked an old sedan beside the road, at the end of the driveway across from Neenah's.

Cody blocked the vehicle in with his squad car and updated dispatch. When he got out, he shined his light through the closest window on the mysterious sedan. A cache of light strings, gigantic bells, and a wire-and-light reindeer occupied the back seat.

He set off for Neenah's house but only made it as far as the road before a white figure materialized in Neenah's driveway with a crinkling shopping bag clutched in one furry hand.

Cody lifted his flashlight. "Police. Stop right there."

The oversized feet stumbled to a standstill. Maybe this would be that easy.

"Put the bag down."

That order, too, brought compliance.

"Interlock your hands behind your head and kneel down—"

The suspect turned and sprinted. Or tried to, until he tripped over his own gigantic footwear.

A grunt preceded a wild scramble to rise. The impractical footwear hindered the effort, so one hand between the shoulder blades returned him to a prone position. Cody caught one furry arm and then the other. With cuffs in place, he helped the yeti to the kneeling position he'd asked for in the first place.

Cody gripped the floof of white hair at the crown of the costume and lifted off the mask. The teenage boy underneath cringed and bowed his head of wild curls. He had seen this kid around but didn't know whether he was a minor or not. First things first, he pulled the script from his pocket and read off his Miranda rights.

The boy confirmed that he understood.

He tucked the card away again. "Do you have an ID on—"

"You saved me!" Pounding footsteps accompanied Kaylie's shout.

Cody shifted to keep an eye on both the unmasked yeti and Kaylie. "Get back inside. I'll get you when it's safe."

Kaylie loped to a stop, eyes fixed on the captive. "Abel?"

"You know this guy?"

"He's friends with Bryce. And, like, everybody." She'd never taken her focus off the boy, and she aimed her next question at him. "Why're you stealing people's decorations?"

"It's kind of a Robin Hood situation." His voice climbed

and fell, as if he couldn't decide whether to be proud of or sorry for his actions.

Cody scoffed. Every criminal was the hero of their own story.

"No, really. We were going to set up an epic display at the nursing home for Christmas. My grandma's in there, and it's the worst. And some of the guys thought so too, so we were, like, working together, and yeah …" His lips skewed, and he fixed a pleading gaze on Kaylie. "When I realized you saw me, I was going to let you in on it, but when I tried to catch up with you, you screamed, and I guess called the cops."

"Oh, I'm so sorry. I had no idea."

"Kaylie—" But neither teen listened to Cody's warning.

"My bad," Abel said. "I didn't even realize this was your house or I wouldn't have come here." His eyes shifted toward Cody. "Too many cops around."

"That's kinda nice, but …" Kaylie scrunched her nose. "It *was* stealing, no matter whose house it was. Is that what your grandma really wants?"

The boy dropped his gaze, the first sign of remorse. The kid had no idea how much trouble he was in.

Cody got Abel's information, relayed what he'd learned to dispatch, then left him in the back of the car as a second cruiser pulled up.

Justin McKinnon got out. "You got a minute?"

"The kid mentioned accomplices. We need to sweep the property."

The task took them in separate directions. When they confirmed via the radio that they'd found nothing, they agreed to meet up back at the house.

Cody reached the side door first and let himself in. If Kaylie hadn't gotten through to Neenah yet, he'd have her call again before he left.

As he advanced down the hallway, his radio blared Quince's voice. "Burglary suspect in custody."

He kneaded the back of his neck. The promotion was Quince's for sure—as if it hadn't been as soon as Cody told his dad to give the job to the competition.

But Kaylie had called in a panic. Coming to her aid wasn't self-sabotage, it was instinct. Loyalty. Sacrifice. He'd make the same call again. He stepped into the living room.

The teen sat on the couch, clutching her phone to her stomach as tears filled her eyes.

No one should've been able to get past him to upset her like this. He'd come expressly to protect her. He hadn't foreseen a threat coming through a phone call. "What is it?"

"Neenah's at the hospital."

Chapter Fourteen

Mustering his last shred of patience, Cody put his hand between Abel's head and the doorframe of Justin's cruiser as he transferred the suspect.

Once the kid was in, Justin pushed the door shut. "I wanted to tell you when I got here, but—"

But Cody had asked for help clearing the property. He lifted a hand to tell Justin he didn't need to apologize. "We had work to do."

Justin didn't look convinced. "I can't believe Quince didn't call you directly about Neenah. We all know ..." He cleared his throat. "You're her emergency contact."

Cody nodded his thanks, both for the willingness to take custody of Abel and the acknowledgement that Quince should've done more than report an anonymous pedestrian had been injured. Surrendering the glory in the burglary case was a lot easier than forgiving Quince for withholding Neenah's identity.

Cody depended on her. Needed her. Would protect her with his life.

He loved her.

Had for years.

Still hadn't told her as much, though. He might not get the chance tonight, but he could be there for her in other ways.

"You've got it from here?"

"Yeah, man. Go." Justin waved him off.

He jogged to his own cruiser, where Kaylie waited in the passenger seat. He pulled onto the road. Her company constituted one reason he might not get the chance to pour his heart out. The other reason, Neenah had a concussion. His job tonight was to deliver Kaylie to her and ensure she received the best possible care. That would have to be enough to relieve some of the relentless pounding in his chest.

"It's bad that they're scanning her head, right?" Kaylie's voice was as quiet and watery as melting snow.

"It's routine. She hit her head and passed out." Details he hated but managed to recite without growling. "They're ruling out the serious possibilities."

"We *hope* it rules them out. It might *prove* them instead."

His bulletproof vest pressed against his chest as if he'd strapped it on too tight. But Kaylie didn't need his concern amplifying hers. He kept a steady grip on the wheel and sped onward, scanning the road for anything that might move into his path. "If that happens, she'll be where they can treat her right away."

"So was my mom."

The useless body armor didn't protect him from the gut punch. He let up on the gas pedal and glanced at his passenger. Streetlights flashed across the elves decorating her pajama pants. Her hair fanned over her shoulders like a shawl. Her face looked small. Defenseless.

She needed comfort.

The Bible had some wordy verse about comfort. God comforted his people in their hardships so they could comfort others with the comfort they received. Or something like that. A whole chain of comfort.

So... what had comforted him, as he'd kneeled over Neenah's broken body?

Nothing. He'd been terrified.

Same with during the ambulance ride.

But as he'd paced the waiting room during the first of multiple surgeries, a snatch of a verse had come to him. He'd looked it up, memorized the whole passage, and repeated it to himself a hundred times or more over the following months.

"'Fear not, for I have redeemed you; I have called you by name, you are mine. When you pass through the waters, I will be with you; and through the rivers, they shall not overwhelm you; when you walk through fire you shall not be burned, and the flame shall not consume you. For I am the Lord your God, the Holy One of Israel, your Savior.' Isaiah 43:1–3."

"Whoa." Kaylie's head shifted back, then she laughed. "That was really weird until I realized it was a verse. You have that whole thing memorized?"

"I memorized it like my life depended on it." Because in some ways, it had.

Kaylie sighed. "She's probably fine, huh?"

"And if she's not, God will go through it with us." His voice deepened with emotion. Hopefully, she wouldn't read it for the fear that it was. He prayed that the Lord would increase his faith to match his words.

Half a block passed in silence. "She loves you too," Kaylie said.

She had a lot more confidence about his standing with Neenah than he did.

"You'll be on my side now, right?" she asked. "She has to stop patrolling. It's dangerous. I've been telling her."

He navigated into the parking lot and as close to the emergency room doors as he could. There, he shut off the engine. He squelched the impulse to run inside and made himself focus on Kaylie. "Justice and public safety are noble callings, and people in those fields get enough pushback as it is. She needs our support."

"But—"

"It's going to take some time for her to work out who she is now that she's not on the force. Like I bet it will for you after moving all the way here. Some things are changing for me, too, and I'm still figuring out my own next steps. It's our job to offer support without limiting each other from reaching for the callings God's given us."

Kaylie scrunched her mouth but didn't argue.

That settled, he hurried toward the building.

Kaylie, runner that she was, bounced along beside him. "What changes have you had?"

No way she wanted to hear about his career. She was fishing for details about him and Neenah, and those weren't his to provide. Not to Kaylie anyway. "I'll let you talk to Neenah."

"I know what *that* means." She managed a hop-skip-kick move he couldn't replicate if he tried.

He also couldn't replicate her confidence. He didn't know where he stood with Neenah or how much damage their fight had done. All he could do was ask to be taken to her at the desk.

A nurse crossing behind the receptionist paused and motioned them to follow her. "She's already given permission for you two. I'll take you right back."

Whatever the answers to the unknowns, it looked like he and Kaylie would be finding out together.

* * *

The fall hadn't killed her, but Cody just might.

Neenah twirled the hospital band on her wrist. She'd meant to never get another one of these for as long as she lived. Or at least for a few decades. Yet, here she was, awaiting the results of a scan to make sure she hadn't broken anything important when she'd slipped and knocked herself out. And all for a stupid reason too.

She'd never felt so lost. *Lord, what am I really supposed to be doing with my life?*

Running through parking lots in the dark certainly wasn't it. But neither was working at Second Chances. With Cody and Kaylie, she felt a sense of rightness. Of home. But she still needed work. Meaningful work that used the gifts she'd been given.

Movement at the doorway signaled the verdict about her head had come in. She folded her fidgeting hands and turned her attention to the door. Instead of a nurse or doctor, however, Cody and Kaylie stepped through.

For them—not to mention for her own sake—she would make changes. Tonight's watch shift had, indeed, been the last patrol of her life. While that grieved her and she was sore from her fall, a sense of peace seeped through her body. God had some other plan for her besides the neighborhood watch and besides Second Chances. She just had to wait long enough to see what He'd reveal, and in the meantime, she wasn't so bad off. Not when she had these two with her.

Cody still wore his uniform. Concern wrinkled his forehead, and his mouth twitched with a half-smile that seemed to say he was glad to see her alert and in one piece.

Kaylie launched herself across the space and threw her arms around her. "I'm so glad you're all right."

As if a lead ball rolled around with each shift of her head, her headache intensified. She mashed her eyes shut.

By the time she opened them again, Cody had a hand on

Kaylie's shoulder, guiding her back. "Let's not assault her until she tells us she's up for it."

"Oh. Sorry." Kaylie bit her lip. "*Are* you okay? I was really worried."

"Yeah." Even speaking shifted the lead ball, and her eyes sank closed for the space of the word. "I have a concussion and a headache. Quiet and calm are the name of the rules."

Kaylie squinted. "Name of the game?"

She hummed to the affirmative, but couldn't muster the energy to say as much.

"Hello, hello." A doctor appeared, and Cody shifted to allow her to approach. "Can we discuss the results of your scans with your company present?"

Neenah started to nod, but her headache stopped her. "Yes. They're family."

Kaylie tipped a smile first at her, then at Cody. He didn't seem to notice; his focus on Neenah didn't waver.

The doctor consulted her tablet. "The CT scan revealed nothing concerning, but because of the concussion, you'll need to be observed for the next twenty-four hours to make sure your symptoms don't get worse."

"I have to stay?"

"Unless you have someone who can keep an eye on you for the next twenty-four hours."

"She does," Cody vowed.

"But your stakeout." She reached to touch his arm, but he was too far away.

He stepped forward and gripped her hand. Suddenly, that became the most comfortable part of her body.

"It's over." His thumb rubbed a gentle circle. "They caught the guy."

"They? Not you?"

"He caught the yeti." Kaylie braced both hands on the bedrail. "It was one of my classmates. Maybe with some of the other guys helping sometimes, I guess? He didn't mean any harm, but he scared me half to death."

"What? When?"

The doctor held up a pen like an orchestra conductor. "Sounds like you all have a lot of catching up to do, but let's get through these directions first. Then, I can discharge you, but everyone has to remember Neenah needs her rest. That includes the mental variety."

They gave her a chorus of *yes, ma'am*s, but as soon as Neenah got the chance, she was grilling them about the night's events. Thanks to the doctor's efficiency, she found no opportunity in the room. A nurse wheeled her toward the exit while Cody went ahead to pull around. From her place in the wheelchair, the climb into the passenger seat of his truck looked like scaling a mountain. She pushed to her feet as Cody got the door for her.

Kaylie hovered by her elbow. "This isn't what we came here in. Where's the police car?"

"Graham swapped things around for me while we were inside."

Neenah was glad they'd thought of it. First, she was trying to trust God had something good in store for her future, but she'd rather not face the reminder of all she would never have again in the form of a ride in a police car. Also, none of the department vehicles were as high as Cody's truck, so for any of those, his hand wouldn't be on the small of her back, helping her in. And none of the squad cars enveloped her in Cody's familiar, comforting scent, like a cashmere blanket warm with spices and vanilla.

She rested heavily in the seat. Her head pounded each time a door closed, but then the rock of the vehicle—or perhaps the knowledge that Cody would take care of her, of everything— lulled her eyes closed.

* * *

In the morning, Neenah's senses, from the emptiness in the pit of her stomach to the smell of hot batter to the low tones of conversation, drew her to the kitchen.

Kaylie bent to peer under the lid of a waffle press. "Are you sure we shouldn't wake her up?"

"Doctor's orders." Cody, in track pants and a T-shirt, rifled through the contents of her fridge door. His hair was mussed from what she assumed, based on the blanket and pillow folded and stacked in the living room, had been a night on the couch.

She'd been looking for purpose, and she'd focused on her career, because that had always stirred the most passion in her. But standing here, observing her strong and handsome best friend and her peppy new ward, still rumpled from sleep as they cooked breakfast and discussed their concern for her, breathed life into longings she'd never allowed herself before.

This was ... well, this could be the start of a family. Her own family.

She braced herself against the table.

Caring for the people God had brought into her life could bring so much of the purpose she'd been seeking. Even once she found a job, knowing her work would benefit her loved ones would add meaning and depth to her days.

"She was still breathing half an hour ago." Cody's announcement meant he'd looked in on her. Probably repeatedly throughout the night.

Here's hoping she hadn't been drooling or snoring.

"The whole reason you're here is because her condition might change." Kaylie fully opened the waffle iron and used a fork to loosen the waffle.

Cody reached farther inside the fridge. "There's no reason to think it will. People recover from concussions all the time."

He straightened and caught sight of Neenah. His lips lifted in an instant smile, the picture of domestic bliss with kind blue eyes, a soft blue T-shirt, and a bottle of maple syrup in his hands.

A memory from the night before stirred. She'd slid off the seat of his truck and into his arms, against his chest. Her forehead had rested on his neck, and his voice reverberated through her body as he instructed Kaylie to move ahead and unlock the house.

After that, she recalled only comfortable darkness.

"You carried me in last night."

He smirked and flexed, but before she could appreciate the view, Kaylie wrapped her in a hug.

"You're awake!"

Neenah winced against the onslaught of movement and sound.

"Sorry," Kaylie whispered. She patted Neenah's shoulder and backed away. "Want waffles?"

"They look amazing."

Kaylie ushered her to the table and helped her sit. She could've managed but didn't have the heart to discourage such sweetness. They delivered everything she needed, and once they joined her with their own waffles, Cody prayed.

Kaylie carried the breakfast conversation. Neenah caught Cody watching her with an intensity that suggested his silence wasn't for lack of having things to say. But he didn't scowl like she deserved after she'd gotten hurt for nothing. Instead, his unfurrowed brow and quiet smiles suggested he might want to make up as badly as she did.

Kaylie swirled her last bite through a puddle of syrup and stuffed it in her mouth. "I was thinking for the white elephant gift exchange with your friends on Saturday, I could give away my old running shoes." She gulped. "You said it's a gag gift, right?"

Neenah pushed away her own empty plate. "It is, but let's throw in a bag of candy, too, so they get something good."

"Oh! Or"—as Kaylie stretched the word, she stood and collected dishes—"there are some rocks by the barn. I could paint a face on one and give that. Would that be funnier? I think it would be."

"You could make it a theme," Cody suggested. "A decorated rock and rock candy."

"I like that idea." She delivered the dishes to the sink.

He stood. "I've got it from here."

"It's no prob—" Her voice trailed off as she looked from one to the other. Her eyes grew big. "Oh! You want alone time. That's fine. I'll clean up. You guys can go ... wherever."

"I called Hollis to find out what BeeBee needs in the morning." Cody returned the maple syrup and milk to the refrigerator. "When I asked how to put on a halter, he said to just make sure she had hay and water and to let you walk me through the rest later." He assessed Neenah. "If you're not up for a walk out there, he said he would come by."

"A walk would be nice." Time alone with Cody, even better. "Let me get changed."

He dipped his head and took the same opportunity, because when she met him by the side door, he'd traded the joggers for jeans and had layered a jacket over the T-shirt. Damp finger tracks and a lack of cowlicks proved that he'd tried to tidy up his hair, but blond stubble marked his jaw. She didn't often see this casual side of him.

She curbed her longing to run her fingers over his jaw. "Thanks for being here."

"Of course." He took her coat from a hook and held it for her.

"You'll have to go in at some point today?" She still didn't have all the details on what had happened, but with suspects in custody on two cases, follow-up would be required.

"Once you and Kaylie are settled for the day." He opened the door and followed her out. "I'll come back as soon as I can."

The fresh snow reflected the morning sun. She squeezed her eyes shut and dipped her chin against the glare.

"Hang on." Cody's footsteps retreated toward the driveway.

She shaded her eyes and cracked her lids open. He collected something from his truck cab and jogged back. He extended sunglasses toward her.

She muttered her thanks and slid them on. "I guess light sensitivity is a real thing with a concussion."

"I'm sure fatigue is too, so let's make this quick." He rubbed her back and motioned toward the barn.

She hesitated because she didn't want to lose his touch, but as she followed one of the well-worn wheel tracks, he settled his arm around her. She leaned into his side. A girl could get used to this. Even an independent and headstrong one like her.

His chest expanded with a deep breath. "Detective was never the role I wanted most from my dad."

She tightened the arm she'd looped behind his waist. "What role do you want?"

"From him?" He stuffed his free hand in his coat pocket, eyes pointed toward their feet kicking through the fresh snow. "Son. But I'm not going to get it. Not in the way I want anyway. Biologically, there's no argument, but I'll never have his approval."

Her composure fractured like an egg. He shouldn't have to give up on obtaining something that should've been his from his very first birthday. "Because someone else made your arrest?"

"That, but also because we have different values. He purposely stood in my way, figuring I'd push back because

'Adams men fight for what they want.'" He intoned an impression of his father's voice. "Unless I didn't want the job or you enough, in which case, I deserved to hit a roadblock."

Or you. He'd slid that in so naturally.

They'd talked about how his dad hadn't been the sole force keeping them apart, but the man had created one more hurdle, and if his motivation had been doubts about Cody's dedication, he didn't know his son at all.

"When did you have this conversation?"

"Yesterday. Right before I got the call about Ernie Schilling and the burglar."

Everything clicked. "And then you came to see me with something to prove."

"I'm sorry." His mouth curved with regret. "It wasn't fair to take that out on you. I know you feel called to the neighborhood watch. I don't want to stand between you and the work the Lord has for you."

"I'm sorry too, because I'm not sure it is my calling. Maybe your objection was one way God was trying to tell me that before I went and made a terrible judgment call." Crazy how her mouth resisted the words, fought to fall silent. But Cody had blazed a trail she had to follow if she wanted this to succeed. "I never should've gotten out of my truck. I was so caught up in being helpful, I didn't look before stepping in front of a moving vehicle, and it was all for nothing."

The truth sounded so awful. She braced for a reprimand.

Instead, Cody stepped ahead and rolled open the barn door. "I haven't heard the full story yet."

"Oh." She'd figured he would've heard the details from Quince or Justin.

Sheltered by the dim barn, she pulled off the sunglasses and slipped them into her pocket. BeeBee whinnied a greeting and stuck her head over the half-door.

Allowing the horse to come between them, Neenah

stroked the mare's nose and recapped what prompted her to follow on foot. Then came the hard part—filling in the details she'd only learned after she'd come to.

"The lights I thought turned off suspiciously were on a timer. The person who moved in the shadows to the parking lot lives above the business. I scared him half to death by stepping out in front of his car—and he wasn't the yeti or the burglar." She risked glancing toward Cody.

Instead of the frustration or judgment she'd feared, the lines of his face communicated support. Concern. "Hindsight's twenty-twenty. What's important is you're okay. Or you will be."

Could making up really be this easy?

BeeBee nudged Neenah's arm, impatient for breakfast. She pointed Cody to the feed bin. "She gets one scoop."

He added the grain to her feeder. When he returned to her in the aisle outside the stall, he wrapped an arm around her shoulders and pulled her in to press a kiss to her forehead.

That was a yes. Reconciliation really was that easy.

She slid her arms around his waist under his jacket, his T-shirt soft against her skin. "Who did the burglar end up being? Someone on your radar?"

"Zane Harris, Tech City's evening manager." His voice rumbled against her cheek as he toyed with her hair.

"Why'd he do it?"

"Quince couldn't get anything out of him." He spoke in the slow cadence of a man thoroughly distracted. He ran his fingers along her scalp and behind her ear, simultaneously pushing her hair back and leaving a trail of heat. "All we know is the tracker led them to his house, and some of the merchandise stolen on previous occasions was in the garage."

"Pretty brazen of him to steal from his own customers." The breathless voice didn't sound like hers. Since when was she more interested in romance than in justice? Oh, who cared? She tucked herself closer to him, where she could enjoy the solid warmth of his embrace.

"My guess is, the more times he got away with it, the braver he got. But …" He cleared his throat. "I might let Quince do the digging into all the details about why and how."

"What?" She arched her back, reestablishing eye contact without breaking the embrace. "Why?"

One side of his mouth hitched, and tenderness filled his eyes. "Because I miss you."

"But …" Confusion could be a symptom of a concussion, but she'd thought she'd been tracking okay up until now. "What does missing me have to do with Quince?"

"I miss working with you." He ran his knuckles along her cheek. "And I'm tired of trying to impress my dad. Like I said, different values. The technical college is looking for more than one criminal justice instructor. I'm going to take one of the positions. I think you should too. We can work together again. Put our experience to good use. Make a difference for the next round of cops."

He would go with her?

Suddenly, the job she'd so hastily refused to pursue shone with new value. With purpose, even. He had a point that instructors could influence their students in ways that would help them throughout their entire careers. Was that what God had for her? And with Cody's company, no less?

"Why would you teach when you can still do the job? You love it."

His thumb skimmed the corner of her mouth, but his gaze locked on hers. "The job isn't my greatest love."

Was the barn swaying? She braced herself against his chest. "You'd do that? Give up the job for me? To keep me company?"

"I would do it for *us*." He kissed her temple, and his breath whispered on her skin as he continued. "Haven't you heard? Adams men fight for what they want."

The back of her neck tingled. "And you want more time with me."

"Among other things." Cody's focus dipped to her lips. "Just one problem."

"What's that?" Her question rode on a half-laugh. She had a very good feeling they could solve this problem.

"I don't want to fight for a kiss." His blue irises searched her face. "I only want it if—"

"I surrender, Officer Adams." She held her hands up, though with his arms around her, her elbows poked his ribs.

His grin flared then sobered as he lowered his head. She understood the shift. Kissing one's best friend was serious business. The still unfamiliar thrill shot straight through her core and fanned to the fingertips of her raised hands. In this embrace, she felt the loyalty and care he'd lived out for years, expressed in a new way she'd been a fool to outlaw for so long.

She'd planned to be a career police officer and spend her life protecting and serving her community. And while she wouldn't have chosen the accident, this moment and many others, including all of those with Kaylie, never would've happened if she hadn't been forced to start over on the hunt for a new purpose in life. God had taken an action meant for evil and used it for good.

And like Cody, who would fight for what he wanted but would draw the line at forcing her participation, God had set the stage and invited her to surrender the last vestiges of her plan. Surrender and wait to see what He'd do next.

Once she had, He'd given her more than she'd thought to ask for herself. Emotion welling, she pulled back just enough for a stuttering breath.

Cody's thumb grazed her lips, and he blinked his eyes open. "Are you okay?"

Heat built behind her eyes, but she nodded. "My plan's out the window."

His Adam's apple bobbed. "Do you miss it?"

Her lips tingling from his kiss, she smiled. "This is going to be so much better."

"Going to be?" His eyebrows lifted in a gentle tease.

"Yeah. Because we're just getting started."

"Ah." His arms encircled her, and his breath tickled her ear. "You have to admit, there's nothing quite like Christmas in Redemption Ridge ... Not a bad time to get hitched."

"Cody." She swatted his chest. "I'm the impulsive one. You're supposed to be the voice of reason."

His shoulders lifted in a playful shrug. "I didn't hear anyone say anything unreasonable."

The sense of purpose she'd experienced in the kitchen that morning *had* been tied to the idea that this would last a lifetime. Still, to get married this Christmas season would mean going from first kiss to vows in a matter of weeks. "It's too soon. At least ..."

"What?" Interest lit his eyes.

"It's too soon to get married. As far as proposals go, I don't need anything fancy, but I do expect a ring. That might take time. And the kneeling thing always sounded kind of ... I don't know. Romantic."

His mouth opened, and his eyebrows dipped for a second. She'd given him a lot to process there.

He licked his lips. "Always? I thought you spent most of your life not wanting to get married."

"I did. But ..." She grinned. "A girl can dream. If we're both all in, we should do it right."

He laughed and pulled her close once more. "I love you."

The heat behind her eyes turned liquid, and tears gathered. "I love you too."

He kissed her forehead and inhaled a deep breath. The

pause in the security of his embrace gave her time to collect her emotions before he looked down at her again with the expression Kaylie had recognized so soon after moving to town.

As the cliché went, he looked at her as if she were the only woman in the world.

Then and there, she made a new plan.

As far as it depended on her, they would spend their days together living out the biggest and best cliché of them all: happily ever after.

Chapter Fifteen

L eave it to Redemption Ridge to rally behind a yeti for the sake of spreading Christmas cheer. In the few days since the arrest, word about Abel's mission spread.

Around Cody, the lawn of the nursing home resembled a Christmas festival. Dozens of residents had gathered to string up lights, tend to the technical aspects of powering and timing the variety of decorations, and build morale.

Cody would've preferred a quiet day with Neenah, allowing her to recuperate from the concussion, but Kaylie had talked them into joining the community. One of his hands already occupied with a drink carrier of hot cocoas, he slowed by The Cakery's table. Justin McKinnon's wife, Caroline, owned the bakery and had been serving up sweet treats all day, though she'd stepped away from the table now. With the sun low on the horizon, the assortment was pretty picked over, but anything Caroline baked was delicious.

Besides, Cody was banking on a warm beverage and sugar to perk up Neenah. Only a couple of days after hitting her head, she probably shouldn't have spent most of the afternoon with the other volunteers, threading lights through arched garden trellises to create a tunnel leading up the front walk.

Eventually, she'd announced she needed to take a seat for a while. Not a good sign. He'd set off in search of refreshments. He needed her to last until twilight, when all the lights would illuminate.

"Hang on!" Arms full with two giant pastry boxes, Caroline hurried from the street, across the trampled snow, and to the sweets table. She set her load in an open space and lifted the top lid with a flourish. "Good things come to those who wait."

A white puff of air slipped from Cody's lips. A few weeks ago, he hadn't been sure, but now he could testify that they really did. *Thank you, Lord.*

The tray of cupcakes sprinkled with peppermint candies didn't compete with the blessing of his relationship with Neenah, but the confections certainly did look good. Still … He lifted the beverage carrier. "I'm not sure how much more goodness I can hold."

The statement rang true on multiple levels.

In the days since he'd apprehended Abel, word of the teen's mission had spread. Of one mind, residents had dropped charges against Abel and his friends and decided to carry out their mission—minus the yeti costumes and thefts. Turned out, when you asked for donations instead of stealing, people would raid their stashes of unused light strings and outdoor décor and supply an overwhelming array of options.

They'd have nothing to show for the effort but a big tangle of lights and bulbs, but hyper-organized Juliana Reynolds kept everyone on track. In twenty minutes or so, they'd enjoy a light show the likes of which had never been seen before in Redemption Ridge—especially considering Cody's plan.

"There's always room for more goodness." Caroline produced a flattened pastry box from beneath her table and deftly flipped and folded until it formed a square large enough for four cupcakes. She glanced at the drink carrier. "Three cupcakes?"

He nodded.

She loaded up the box, passed it over, then helped set the beverage carrier on top. "Merry Christmas."

"Merry Christmas." He headed toward where he'd left Neenah and Kaylie.

The punch of a snowball hit his shoulder blade. He froze, praying the hot cocoas wouldn't go tumbling. When they didn't, he adjusted his grip and turned to find his attacker.

Gideon Reynolds, a long-time friend who was also in on the proposal, dusted his hands and jogged up. "You are not making this easy."

Cody cut a glance toward Neenah. She sat at what they'd dubbed the Command Center, where Gary Jones, hoping to prove himself so Tech City would rehire him, put his technological skills to use setting some of the lights to music. Clive had already hinted he'd give the guy a second chance.

He refocused on Gideon. "Not making what easy?"

"Proposal planning."

"It's planned." He dropped his voice to avoid broadcasting the details to all of Redemption Ridge. Neenah shouldn't be the last person to know what he was up to tonight. "When the lights come on, you, Hollis, and Justin are clearing the tunnel. I've got the rest."

He'd called her dad, picked a ring, and memorized a script. As long as he could remember it, everything was set.

"Yeah?" Gideon crossed his arms. "Who's taking pictures?"

"Pictures?" Neenah hadn't mentioned those in her short list of wishes.

"It's a thing. You're supposed to have a photographer

hiding out nearby to capture the big moment. Girls expect stuff like that."

Cody could only shrug. "Neenah's not sentimental."

"About this she will be. Don't worry. I got you covered. Lucy said she'll take some, and if she can make those cows of hers look good, you'll be fine."

He should probably be insulted, but the logic tracked. A veterinarian, Lucy had created a social media account for her two miniature cows and amassed a significant following. And as Hollis's wife, Lucy had likely also known the plan, so Gideon hadn't spread the word beyond the small circle of confidence.

"Okay. Thanks." He shifted to step away.

"It's Hollis who won't carry his weight."

Cody cocked his head. Hollis wasn't the type to back out of a simple task like clearing the tunnel. "How so?"

"He says he's got a white horse, but he refuses to bring it so you can ride up in style because you're a scaredy-cat."

That sounded more like fun-seeking Gideon than even-keeled Hollis, who'd never given him a hard time about not enjoying horseback riding. "No one's riding in on a white horse. And while we're at it, I don't want a flash mob, a special appearance by Santa Claus, or anything involving police."

"Okay. None of that. I promise." He held up a hand as if to take an oath.

That sounded like a half-truth. Whatever he had planned, it wasn't one of the three ideas Cody had come up with. "It's low-key, okay? Neenah's not one for a bunch of frills."

"Sure. No frills, either. How do you feel about snow?"

He shot a look skyward. A few wisps of clouds floated high in the atmosphere, but nothing hinted at precipitation.

Gideon stepped away. "See you on the other side."

Cody stood frozen, blinking after him. Under other circumstances—like when his entire future wasn't on the line

—Gideon's antics amused him. But for all the crazy ideas, the guy had a good heart and his friends' best interests in mind. Choosing to believe that whatever he had planned would turn out all right, Cody resumed his course, only to pull up short when he nearly smashed his load into a man's chest.

Chief eyed the to-go cups but saved his real ire for Cody. "You applied for the instructor position at the college."

Clinging to his dad's arm, his mom offered a sweet smile.

"I did." The same day he and Neenah had discussed working there together. What he hadn't done was share his plans. He'd been waiting to hear he got the job before he told anyone, including his mother.

But he'd known all along that his father had connections. Most likely, those extended to the college. Hopefully, the ties weren't strong enough to block a career change.

Chief's glare didn't let up. "Why would you do that when you just earned detective?"

His mom's smile broadened.

Cody looked from her to his father's stony countenance. "Because I haven't."

"It takes time for paperwork to go through." He lifted a hand as if to wave a stack of forms. "I knew Neenah was impulsive. I didn't think you were."

His mom tweaked Cody's elbow. "I'm so proud of you."

At least one of them was. If only he could focus on her, but he and his dad needed to settle the ongoing tension between them. If such a thing were possible, and he prayed it was, he needed to confront reality. "I can only think of one reason you'd want me to get detective now."

"The fact that you solved two cases?"

"Two?" He'd made one arrest, and that not even on his own case. He'd only been on the scene because he happened to know Kaylie.

"The Christmas decoration thief and the home burglar."

"I didn't catch the burglar."

"That was your operation. Even if you didn't make the arrest, your stakeout solved the case."

"I heard all about it." His mom patted Chief's arm as if he was the source of her information. "What a smart setup, the way you had the homeowner talk about going out of town and how the house sitter couldn't arrive until the next morning. It all worked so beautifully."

As unbelievable as it was, she must've gotten those details from his father. So now, suddenly, his dad was praising his work? He ought to feel the satisfaction he'd been chasing for years, but instead, frustration built like the whine of a distant siren speeding closer. "Sounds like a good note to go out on, then."

The sun dropped below the horizon. Strings of lights blinked on. Pretty soon the tunnel would illuminate, and he had places to be.

He brought his focus back in time to see his mother stepping away from Chief. "I'll give you two a minute."

Cody took a breath to tell her not to bother, but then his father spoke.

"I was too hard on you. I wish you'd stay."

He watched his mother disappear into the crowd. Without her, this conversation was likely to fall flat faster than Abel the Yeti. But he could give it another minute, just in case. "You *wish* I'd stay, or you're going to find a way to make me?"

His father dusted his coat sleeve. "If the college job is what you want, I won't stop you."

"It is."

Chief frowned and nodded. "And Neenah?"

Beyond his father, she stood a few feet from the Command Center, poised with a question on her face. She wanted to know if he needed backup.

"I love her." He stepped around the chief. He had a plan

to execute that needed to happen at dusk, and already the first few stars had appeared in the sky above.

"I know I won't be disappointed," his father's voice trailed him.

Again, he stopped. Turned back. "By what?"

His dad swallowed hard. "The recruits I get from your classes at the college. I know they'll be the best the department's seen." In the plain struggle to meet Cody's eyes, humility shone. "Aside from you, of course."

He didn't outright claim to be proud of Cody, but as far as compliments went, those were good. More goodness to pile onto the stack of it growing in his life.

He dipped his chin. "Thanks, Chief."

"Perhaps, since you won't be working with me in that capacity moving forward, you could call me ... something else, Son." He punctuated the stilted statement with a small, helpless smile.

Son. The role he'd wanted. His for the taking.

Accepting it meant forgiving his dad for the painful years of unreasonable expectations, but the joy blazing through him wouldn't have it any other way. No longer working together might be a fresh start for them. A way to see each other in new light, to go back to being father and son without the power dynamic that had developed over Cody's years on the force. "Sure, Dad. I'll see you and Mom for Christmas."

His father nodded and waved.

The tunnel illuminated. Thousands of white bulbs faded in and out like fireflies in perfect formation. Cody beelined for Neenah.

"What did he want?" she asked as she slipped her hot cocoa from the carrier.

"He heard I applied at the college. Sounds like he expects us both to get the job."

"Huh. I guess that's something."

Cody couldn't dwell on that now, as he saw his friends blocking both entrances to the tunnel of lights. Actually... Only Hollis and Justin were on the job. That meant Gideon was up to something else.

Graham stood with his family near the closer entrance, by Hollis and Lucy. To the casual observer, the couples were visiting, but Hollis stepped away from the group when someone approached the tunnel. After a few seconds, the would-be visitor walked away. How long would that last?

Cody set the remaining cupcakes and cocoa on the Command Center table and texted Graham.

CODY

Gideon's up to something. Check on him?

GRAHAM

On it.

With that confirmation, Cody lifted Neenah's cup from her hands.

"Hey." She reached to reclaim it.

"I want to show you something. Come on." He extended his hand to her. "It'll only take a minute."

His tone must've clued her in that the detour was important, because she took his offered hand. By then, Graham had already disappeared into the crowd.

Neenah leaned her head against Cody's shoulder.

"Are you tired? Do I need to get you home?"

"I'm okay for a few more minutes."

He wrapped his arm around her.

As they reached the entrance to the tunnel, his friends quietly moved aside to let them pass. The twenty-foot-long tunnel of lights hemmed them in with a warm glow that blocked out everything beyond its walls.

Still leaning against his arm, Neenah eyed the lights

arching overhead. "This is pretty amazing, isn't it? What people can build when they come together?"

If that wasn't the perfect segue as they reached the center of the tunnel, he didn't know what would be. He stopped walking and faced her, but she lifted a hand like she was feeling for raindrops. "It's snowing. That's ..." Her laugh held wonder. "It's kind of magical, isn't it? The lights, the snow."

Gideon's cryptic comments fell into place. The guy must've acquired a snow machine. He couldn't imagine how he'd set it up without Cody noticing. Hoisted it into a tree or something? He laughed at the thought, and Neenah squeezed his hand, reminding him he had a more important question to focus on.

Working inside his pocket, he opened the ring box and hooked the engagement ring with his index finger. With it curled into his palm, he moved back from Neenah and lowered to one knee. Her attention dropped from the lights and snow that formed a halo around her, and her grip on his fingers tightened.

This was it. The next step toward what he'd been waiting —and fighting—for, a testament to God's faithfulness in working even when progress felt like it was at a standstill.

He lifted the ring. "Neenah ..." His thick throat forced him to pause, swallow, try again. "Neenah, you're my best friend. I can always count on you to have my back, and I hope you know you can always count on me."

She nodded. He'd never seen her look this way, simultaneously so close to crying and grinning.

"You asked me once who you're supposed to be now, in this season of your life, and I said you're still who you've always been—the brave and intelligent Neenah Casper. And you are those things. I admire you for it. But I need to ask if you'd consider changing that last part, because I'd love for you to become the brave and intelligent Neenah Adams."

Her smile bit into her cheeks, and she swiped away tears.

"Neenah, will you marry me?"

She nodded four times, blinking and palming away tears. "Yes."

Cheers and whistles rose from beyond the lights as Cody slid the ring onto her finger. Kaylie had helped him determine the correct size, and Lucy and Piper had helped pick the design. Still, a relieved breath puffed from his lungs when it fit perfectly.

She lifted her hand and wondered at it. He'd chosen well, then. Her watery gaze shifted to him. She tugged him to his feet and met him with a kiss—and not a shy we're-in-public peck either.

She was brave, after all.

He held her face in his hands and kissed her back. She tasted like hot cocoa and dreams come true. All the years of waiting melted like snowflakes, leaving them with all the goodness they could hold.

* * *

Now to him who is able to do far more abundantly than all that we ask or think, according to the power at work within us, to him be glory in the church and in Christ Jesus throughout all generations, forever and ever. Amen.
Ephesians 3:20–21, ESV

Ready for more?

Christmas in Redemption Ridge Series

Year 1
Marrying the Rancher's Daughter
(Jason and Cassie)
By Tara Grace Ericson

Remembering the Rancher
(Maverick and Annabella)
By Liwen Y. Ho

Year 2
Amending the Christmas Contract
(Levi and Ruby)
By Hannah Jo Abbott

Wooing the Widower
(Chaz and Margie)
By Elle E Kay

Year 3

Dreaming About Forever
(Jordan and Alicia)
By Mandi Blake

Bidding on a Second Chance
(Graham and Piper)
By Emily Conrad

Year 4

Marrying the Billboard Cowboy
(Zeke and Kaitlyn)
By Tara Grace Ericson

Healing the Cowboy
(Clint and Nora)
By Mandi Blake

Year 5

Matchmaking the Cowboy
(Hollis and Lucy)
By Emily Conrad

Caring for the Cowboy's Baby
(Dawson and Liberty)
By Hannah Jo Abbott

Year 6

Doting on His Best Friend
(Milo and Phoebe)
By Liwen Y. Ho

Corralling the Cowboy

(Ethan and Bethany)
By Elle E. Kay

Year 7

Keeping the Cowboy's Promise
(Wyatt and Rachel)
By Hannah Jo Abbott

Fulfilling Her Christmas Wish
(Trevor and Lottie)
By Liwen Y. Ho

Year 8

Playing for Keeps
(Justin and Caroline)
By Mandi Blake

Marrying the Accidental Groom
(Gideon and Juliana)
By Tara Grace Ericson

Year 9

Clearing the Cowboy's Name
(Rowan and Penelope)
By Elle E. Kay

Risking His Heart
(Cody and Neenah)
By Emily Conrad

Heroes of Freedom Ridge Series

Looking for more stories with Christmas, community, and

sweet happily ever afters? Visit Freedom Ridge and discover eighteen more faith-filled stories of Christmas in Colorado.

Join in all the fun at our Facebook Reader Group
www.facebook.com/groups/freedomridgereaders
For sneak peeks, giveaways, and tons of Christmas romance fun!

**A sweet small-town romance exclusively for Emily's
email subscribers.**

Food trailer owner Asher has seen too many tears he couldn't
dry. Determined to be part of the solution, he avoids romance
and all the heartbreaking drama that comes along with it.

At least, that's the plan until his heart decides it has a mind
of its own. If he can't rein it in, he's destined to break not one,
but two women's hearts.

Sign up for email newsletters at emilyconradauthor.com
and receive *Between The Two of Us*, the prequel novella to the
Rhythms of Redemption Romances, as a welcome gift.

Also By Emily Conrad

The Rhythms of Redemption Romances

To Bring You Back

An Awestruck Christmas Medley

To Belong Together

To Begin Again

To Believe in You

The Many Oaks Romances

Now or Never

A Surefire Love

A Faithful Protector

Acknowledgments

It's been so good to spend another season in Redemption Ridge. Thank you to my fellow authors for inviting me to this series! What a wonderful couple of years this has been.

I had some help getting Cody and Neenah's story ready for its debut. Thanks to Jessica Kate, for getting involved early with the blurb, which in turn helped me think through the premise. For help with the manuscript itself, my thanks go out to: Janet Ferguson, Jessica Johnson, Maria Thouron, Judy DeVries, Brandi Aquino, Sarah Strong, Jessica Bradley, Jane Bradly, and Kendra Arthur. You caught errors big and small and helped make this story the best it could be.

Thank you, readers, for your years of support and enthusiasm. Without you, Redemption Ridge wouldn't be what it is.

Finally, thank you, Lord, for filling my life with so much goodness.

Emily Conrad writes contemporary Christian romance that explores life's relevant questions. Though she likes to think some of her characters are pretty great, the ultimate hero of her stories (including the one she's living) is Jesus. She lives in Wisconsin with her husband, an energetic coonhound rescue, and two lop-eared bunnies. Learn more about her and her books at emilyconradauthor.com.

facebook.com/emilyconradauthor

instagram.com/emilyrconrad